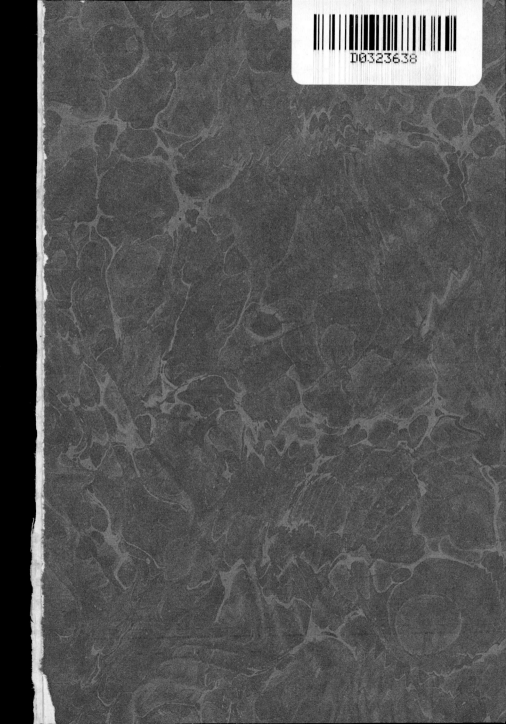

Primrose
Past

———◆◆◆———

For Brenda
       Fulkerson
Hope you enjoy
my "Cygnet"

Caroline Rose Hunt

Primrose Past

The 1848 Journal
of Young Lady Primrose

Caroline Rose Hunt

ReganBooks
An Imprint of HarperCollinsPublishers

HarperCollins books may be purchased for educational, business, or sales promotional use. For information please write: Special Markets Department, HarperCollins Publishers Inc., 10 East 53rd Street, New York, NY 10022.

FIRST EDITION

Designed by Betty Lew

Illustrations inspired by period works of art collected in English Naive Painting (1750–1900) by James Ayres (Thames and Hudson, 1980).

Printed on acid-free paper

Library of Congress Cataloging-in-Publication Data
Hunt, Caroline Rose.
    Primrose past: the 1848 journal of young Lady Primrose / Caroline Rose Hunt.—1st ed.
        p.   cm.
    Fictional re-creation of a 19th century English girl's diary.
    ISBN 0-06-039413-7
    1. Great Britain—History—Victoria, 1837–1901—Fiction.   2. Teenage girls—Fiction.   I. Title.
    PS3558.U46749 P75   2001
    813'.6—dc21   00-047018

01 02 03 04 05 ❖/RRD 10 9 8 7 6 5 4 3 2 1

Summer of 1991

It was a warm day, even for Dallas. Vivian Young, my partner in Lady Primrose's antique shop and tearoom, and I had just finished lunch: she her favorite chicken salad and fruit and I my usual Bombay chicken sandwich with apple and English walnut salad. We were lingering over a pot of our Secret Garden tea as we discussed our upcoming shopping trip to England.

Vivian was leafing through the accumulated mail when she stopped suddenly. "Here's an announcement of a house sale in Herefordshire," she exclaimed. "It's taking place while we're in England. And the house is named Primrose Hall! Can you believe it?" We were both astonished; neither of us had known there was a country house by that name.

The name was, of course, the reason for our interest. When we had first opened our shop in 1987, we had decided to call it Shopping English Countryside. To pique the curiosity of our potential customers, on our very first buying trip to England we had sent two thousand hand-penned postcards reading: "Having a wonderful time. Shopping English Countryside. See you in October. Love, Lady Primrose." We knew of no Lady Primrose. It was simply a name we picked out of the blue because it sounded so very British.

To solve the mystery of the postcard, we extended the invitations for the celebration of the opening of our shop in the name of Lady Primrose. And the name stuck. In the end, no one remembered Shopping English Countryside, but they couldn't forget Lady Primrose. A year later we formally changed the name to Lady Primrose's.

Along with the notice of the sale came a copy of an article from the *Times* of London with additional information. The house, it explained, had been built in 1770 by William Henry Primrose, the third Baronet of Chatfield. Since 1866 it had been owned by the family of the current owners, who were being forced to liquidate the estate to satisfy the 70 percent death taxes required by the British government.

The sale was receiving this unusual media attention because letters from several famous literary figures of the nineteenth century had been discovered in a box in the attic. These were being held for an auction to take place later at Sotheby's in London.

The announcement listed period furniture as well as centennial pieces and an extensive selection of decorative and utilitarian objects.

We had never shopped in Herefordshire and were surprised that an auction would be conducted in a location that remote from London. But Primrose Hall compelled us, and we decided the event sounded well worth the travel time required.

Two months later we were in England. The first two days we spent working with a toiletries house, finalizing the formula for the Lady Primrose's amenities for The Lanesborough, a new luxury hotel under construction in the old St. George's Hospital. Rosewood Hotels & Resorts, which my children and I had established eleven years prior, had been awarded the management contract.

The toiletries house, in business since 1677, had graciously allowed us access to their archives to aid us in our creation of an old-fashioned, all-natural product whose fragrance would be suitable for both sexes. The formula we selected was an updated version of a honey-based recipe, with the addition of royal jelly, an expensive ingredient known to be restorative to the skin.

The day of the Primrose Hall auction, we rose early for our long drive into the countryside. Traffic on the motorway was bumper to bumper coming into the city, and we were relieved that we were going the opposite direction.

Once we turned off onto the auxiliary two-lane roads, our progress was slowed. We passed through several small towns, and then the roads seemed narrower than ever—especially when passing farm vehicles required us to pull to the side of the road. Gradually the terrain changed: gently rolling hills offered us a vista of golden fields, demarcated with hedgerows or stone fences. After several nervous consultations with our map to be sure we really were on the right road, we were reassured when we came across signs directing the public to the auction.

The imposing entrance gates of the property were of wrought iron centered with a coat of arms topped by a leaping stag. With a sigh of relief, we consulted our watches—the auction had not yet begun.

Inside the estate gates we passed a tiny chapel within a walled churchyard filled with moss-covered gravestones. Our journey had taken longer than anticipated, and we were sorry to find we would have no time to visit the charming site.

We were directed to drive off into a field to park, and to proceed to the marquee to register. A tree-canopied drive led us to the house and to a tent that had been erected outside the house for the purpose of the auction. In the tent large screens were erected to facilitate the bidding; there was still time for a brief viewing, so we completed the registration processing, paid for our catalogs, and hurried on to the house.

Primrose Hall is of classic Palladian design, small but of perfect proportions. It was not one of the massive great houses one can visit in England, and I found it all the more pleasing as a result; I felt I could actually enjoy living there. Above the entrance was a stone carved with the numerals 1770. As I opened the door, with its great iron knocker, I felt a sense of intrigue and wonder, as though I had stepped back into 1770.

We entered a large entry hall where many of the objects brought from the upper floors were being exhibited. On one side of the hall was a large living room, which led to the dining room and kitchen; the latter seemed to have been converted from another use, its appliances circa 1920. On the other side was a book-filled, wood-paneled library and another room, possibly an office, with its own outside entryway. Across the entire back of the house ran a narrow gallery, whose windows looked out on a garden. Though now long neglected, it had once been laid out in a formal design. Remnants of a maze were visible, and its topiary bushes were so overgrown the original shapes were unidentifiable. At the focal point in the middle of the garden was a large obelisk covered with hieroglyphics. The main building was flanked with two wings probably built at a later date, as the architectural detail differed from that in the central portion of the house. I was so busy enjoying the house that I almost forgot to look at the furnishings that filled the entire bottom floor of the home.

Remembering our mission, I turned my attention to the furniture, much of which had been removed from the upper floors to the gallery and large entry hall. Among the items was a small Queen Anne secretary bookcase that caught my eye. I squeezed back between the crowded furniture to look it over carefully, but when I found that the slant top lid was locked, and I was unable to examine the interior, I dismissed any thought of bidding upon it.

The auction had attracted a large crowd. Some families had even brought picnic baskets and were enjoying an outing in the once-beautiful grounds of the estate. There were no longer grazing sheep to mow the grass in the meadows, but several of the more adventurous auction attendees had waded through the tall grass to the lakes. In the distance one group in a festive mood picnicked in the ruins of a pagoda with a sharply pointed roof, its once-shining tiles now covered in moss. I recognized the building as what was called a folly, but quite the most unusual folly I'd ever seen. We had constructed a folly in Lady Primrose's after learning of the popularity of these structures, which the English landscape architects utilized to give perspective to their vistas.

By this time we were quite hungry, but with time pressing we contented ourselves with a cup of tea and scones that were for sale next to the marquee. Vivian returned to the viewing, and I went into the marquee to secure seats.

The auctioneer mounted the dais and tested the microphone; it was time for the auction to commence. A newcomer to British auctions, I bid shyly on some ceramic milk pails decorated with the classical facade of the house, bowing out when I reached the limit I had set for myself. I later learned that the two casually dressed men who had outbid me were in the dairy business and well-known collectors of "dairyana."

I watched quietly as other bidders raised fingers, touched their noses, or simply nodded. Still feeling timid, I successfully reentered the competition when a shoe-shaped copper container was offered. Later research revealed that its original use had been for warming ale; its rarity made it significantly more valuable than my modest bid. When Vivian rejoined me, we successfully bid on a large high-backed settle and three feet of old leather-bound books. Though we had been attracted to them for their beautiful leather bindings, we were pleased to find among them early-nineteenth-century editions of authors such as Shakespeare, Chaucer, Milton, Spenser, Sir Isaac Newton, Sir Thomas Browne, and, of course, the classic Greek and Roman authors in their original texts. As the auction progressed we were successful in acquiring several very interesting decorative objects along with a lovely worktable of many naturally colored woods with intricate inlay design of the type from Tunbridge Wells.

When the items from the children's wing came up, I again felt an attraction—indeed, a curiosity—for the unusually small Queen Anne double bonnet secretary bookcase I had spied earlier. The door mirrors were smoky with age, and the walnut wood had a lovely warm patina. Even though I had not been able to examine the interior, I decided I had to have it— not for our shop, but for my own bedroom! I lost all sense of caution and bid eagerly against several other interested parties. When the gavel came down, it was mine, and I felt like a winner despite the fact that my bid significantly exceeded the estimate.

It was six weeks before our container of purchases was scheduled to arrive in Houston. Knowing that late August is a time for storms in the North Atlantic, we were nervous about its crossing. But finally, only a week late, we received the call from our agent that the ship had docked in Houston and had been cleared by customs. Luckily, only one or two items suffered minor damages, and within ten days our acquisitions were on the floor of our antique shop.

The secretary bookcase, I was thrilled to see, arrived without mishap. Before placing it in my own bedroom, I tried keys from our box of miscellaneous keys at the shop. Miraculously one fit; the ball turned, and for the first time I saw the interior of my delightful purchase. It was a lovely example of late-eighteenth-century or early-nineteenth-century craftsmanship. The fittings were all in beautiful condition. There were small drawers suitable for pens and incidentals, slots for letters and papers, and even two little shelves that could be pulled out for candlesticks. The unfaded interior looked as if it had been locked tight for a hundred years.

Several days later, when I found the time, I took pleasure in cleaning and waxing the desk myself. As I was applying the beeswax polish that I had purchased in London, I noticed that the writing surface seemed loose. Knowing that many of the custom-made eighteenth-century furnishings harbored concealed compartments, I carefully applied a little pressure. The whole surface slid back to reveal a compartment and within I discovered a treasure: a host of personal items, clearly quite old but as fresh as the day they were left behind.

I carefully removed the items hidden within: a small partially filled sketchbook; a handful of letters still bearing fragments of sealing wax; a lovely Victorian-style valentine with a sentimental verse inscribed "To My Moonbeam"; and a book with a coat of arms crested with a leaping stag printed in gilt on the cover—the same coat of arms we had seen on the entrance gates to Primrose Hall. Turning its pages revealed its origins: it was a daily journal written in 1848. I wondered if mine were the first eyes to read these words in nearly a century and a half.

Neat penmanship in purple ink filled both sides of each page. On most of the pages the carefully formed letters made it easy to read, but there were places where the handwriting became less careful and required a magnifying glass to decipher the words. I began to leaf through the book—and was engrossed at once by the heartfelt confidences captured there.

It was a rainy afternoon, so I immediately settled down to enter not just a time long past but the world of an endearing young girl at a turning point in her life.

And what I discovered along the way left me intrigued— no, mesmerized—at the story she told, and the mystery it held. Allow me to acquaint you with the young Lady Primrose.

Sister with Goliath

Dear Diary,

Today is my fifteenth birthday. The entire household gathered in the withdrawing room to extend good wishes. Goliath followed along with Papa. Being big even for a Mastiff, Goliath greeted William so exuberantly that he knocked him to the ground. He then licked his face to apologize. William cried loudly, as he does when Mother is present. Mother wiped his tears away and firmly reminded Papa that the withdrawing room is off limits for smelly old Goliath. Papa returned our reluctant dog to the kennel cupboard in the back hall. I was disappointed that he could not stay. Last year, since we took our tea in the garden, Goliath was allowed to attend. Dearest Sister had made a garland of flowers for him to wear. Sister had a way with animals. Her calm and gentle way gave composure to everyone. Though she is absent, she is present still. Simply remembering something she said or did brings her back to me.

Cook baked me her specialty, a rose geranium cake. Mrs. Taylor made a gown for my doll just like one of my own. Of course I'm too old to play with dolls, but I would like to design a whole wardrobe for my doll and have Mrs. Taylor make them, as she is such an excellent dressmaker. William gave me a bottle containing a beetle he had found in the garden. Nanny gave me a copy of Mrs. Hemans's <u>Poems</u>. (She does not know that I slip Mother's novels out of her library and read them when I go to bed. She still thinks of me as a child though I am not.) Cousin Hubert, ever the vicar, gave me a book of daily devotions. Abigail picked me a bouquet of sweet peas, which she remembered are my favourite flowers. Liz made me a pot of paste out of flour and water saying I could use it for découpage. I blurted out that it is of insufficient strength for that purpose, but I immediately regretted my comment because it was thoughtful of her to make me a gift. I quickly whispered to her that I will use it to make a scrapbook of pictures of interest to William for his birthday. Even Clive wove me an ornament out of good old Bess's mane. I think I'll ask Papa to have it made into a brooch, to remind me always of my dearest Bess.

Papa gave me an enameled gold locket that has, on one side, a miniature painted on ivory of his sister Emma, who died in the Virgin Islands in the West Indies. On the other side, behind glass, is a lock of her blond hair. Her eyes were blue like mine. Her face was soft and round. A riband holding a cameo was tied around her graceful long neck. I had never seen her picture before and it made me sad for she looks like Dearest Sister, except that Amy's hair was dark. Papa told me to take great care of it. He was very kind to give me his locket because I know it is something he treasures.

Mr. Austin-Brown gave me a dictionary with the suggestion that I learn daily the spellings and definitions of three words. This seemed like only an assignment in disguise, and I fear my face displayed my thoughts because as if upon impulse he took a folded paper out of his pocket and handed it to me saying, "And I've written a poem for you." Papa insisted he read it aloud so everyone could enjoy it. He hesitated but took it back from my hand and unfolded it. His face heightened in colour when he read it, and his voice was tense. Papa frowned and stroked his chin, as he does when he is thinking. A flush crept up under his tan but he politely said, "That's a beautiful poem, well written. I'd like to submit it for publication." With that, he took it from Mr. Austin-Brown's hand, folded it, and put it in his waistcoat pocket. I later heard him whisper to Mother, "I fear the man has read too much Shelley and Byron; he is an incurable romantic." I really felt it was my poem and Papa should at least have asked my permission, but then he has only the best of intentions. I'm sure if anyone can get it published, he will be able to do so. I felt such compassion for Mr. Austin-Brown's acute discomfort that I gave scant attention to the meaning of the poem and remember little but that he made reference to Venus with skin soft and tender as the down on a white soul-swan.

William, still the spoiled baby even if he is five years old, started crying and whining because he didn't get any presents. Papa, to keep him from ruining my birthday, reached behind William's ear and pretended to find a coin, a gold crown with the profile of Her Royal Highness minted only this year. I don't think William appreciated either Papa's adroitness or the valuable coin, but he did stop crying.

My gift from Mother was you, dear diary. Mother says she started keeping a journal when she was my age and she cherishes the memories preserved there. She made me promise to write at least one thing I've learned each day.

Mother cautioned me to be mindful that, as penmanship indicates character and whether one is a person of worth and education, I must be careful to the point of fastidiousness. I promised her I would write in my very best script, though I despair of ever being able to form my letters as perfectly as she does. When I was learning to make my letters Nanny bound my hand to assist me in developing beautiful penmanship, all to no avail. She says I will never be able to form my letters properly writing with my left hand and so I always try to use my right, unless I'm in a hurry.

Cousin Hubert advised, "Your journal must chart your spiritual progress." Papa said, "Record the little, simple, seemingly unimportant everyday joys of life so that they are not lost." Mrs. Potts declared in her bombastic voice, "Have gratitude for your capacity to enjoy, especially treats from my kitchen." And then she cackled like a hen that has just laid an egg. Nanny didn't give me any instructions, for once, but I know she was probably thinking, "Be honest and confront your bad habits."

William asked Papa why our family coat of arms, which is printed in gilt on the cover, is topped by a leaping stag. Papa explained that the stag is considered a symbol of good luck, but as the coat of arms was created so very long ago he didn't really know why. Then he laughed and added that he guessed our ancestors must have been great at the hunt even before there were guns.

Papa explained that the reason the primrose in our coat of arms is similar to the Tudor rose is that the baronetcy was awarded by a Tudor king. Then he chuckled again and told me that among the many varieties of primroses is the cowslip, which comes up between the cow dung. As our lineage has no actual royal blood, he figured it was good enough for our family.

I commented that we must be of Roman ancestry, as our family motto, "Virtus, Veneratio, Veritas," is in Latin. Papa explained that most family mottoes are in Latin. His eyes twinkled as he said, "That's so the descendants who don't wish to live up to the mottoes can claim they can't read Latin." His voice then took on a serious tone as he explained that our motto means "Virtue, Honor, Trust" and he has always tried to live by those principles, which is more than he could say for some Tudors. In fact, the first Tudor king, Henry VII, was born out of wedlock, a fact he could not condone. And certainly he could not approve of King Henry VIII and his ease of discarding wives.

The Tudors can trace their ancestry back to a Roman Celtic chief who held sway in Colchester over a thousand years ago—Old King Cole, the same merry old soul in William's

Nursery Rhyme Book. Mother smiled to hear Papa recall that, and then commented that the nursery rhyme must have been written long after King Cole lived, as the merry old soul called for his pipe and there was no tobacco on our island a thousand years ago. Papa said that though he was certain it was written long after the real King Cole lived, it was possible that the pipe referred to a flute, but he pointed out that there were no fiddles that long ago. Then I remembered that Nero is said to have played his fiddle as he watched Rome burn, and said so. Nanny frowned and I knew she was thinking I shouldn't contradict my elders, but Papa chuckled and said, "Good for you, Cygnet. And I think this proves the saying, 'Believe nothing you hear, half that you read and even question what you see.'" I love a cheerful temper like Papa's.

I'm thankful today that so many people remembered my birthday. Mother even let me eat the second piece of cake although she usually reminds me ladies are to eat lightly and daintily and never finish every bite on their plate. William can eat anything he wants.

Mother takes pride in the fact that her waist is still as small as it was when she married Papa.

Though it was a dull rainy day, it was a beautiful day to me.

Dear Diary,

Papa went to the village fair today. I asked him to take me with him. He refused. He said he would take me the next time but this time he would be too busy to look after me, as he was showing his best sow and one of his bulls. He has been feeding them extra rations for months so that they would gain as much weight as possible. Papa is proud of the stocky body of Sir Jacob, his red bull with the bald face. He was calved from a cow named Britannia, who received the prize for best cow in milk at the first Royal Show at Oxford. Last year his bull failed not only to receive a blue ribbon but any ribbon at all. Papa said that since a <u>Hereford Herd Book</u> has been published by Mr. T. C. Eyton, the judges will have to take account of Sir Jacob's rare wealth of flesh.

I was sorely disappointed and I fear I wheedled and begged to go, but Papa was firm. I ran upstairs to my room and slammed the door, forgetting all about Mother's poor head. I hope I haven't caused her to have one of her headaches. I felt remorse for my lack of restraint. I threw myself on the bed and wept for a long, long time.

Papa came home in high spirits because his bull had taken the prize as the Grand Champion. He also had been successful in his wagers on the races. Papa's sow did not take a prize, but Papa said that it was for the best because the other farmers

Sir Jacob

Papa's championship sow

need encouragement so that they will continue to work to improve their stock.

He brought me a fairing he had won in a contest. The figurine is a wedding couple standing in front of a castle looking very happy. Papa said it was made in Staffordshire, where many of the pot houses are located.

He encountered his friend, Lord Lyon, who had recently purchased a four-year-old stallion by Bay Middleton, winner of the Epsom Derby in 1836 and one of the most famous sire lines. The stallion's bloodlines on the female side traced back to Snorting Bess, the justly famous mare in the days of King Charles II. Beguiled by this illustrious breeding, his friend had parted with 170 guineas for the horse—no mean sum, Papa says. Alas, to Lord Lyon's great distress, he has not been able to calm the spirited thoroughbred sufficiently to work with hounds, nor to restrain him from bolting at the sound of the hunting horn. Papa offered to bring him to our stable to let Clive work with him because Clive has exhibited great success with horses, even more than Tom. I'm sure Clive will be made a groom one day.

Papa took me to the stable to see the new horse. His name is Thunder. He is a beautiful horse, bay in colour. Papa pointed out that his blood shows in his Arabian head, high croup, and well-set tail. As I drew near, his legs became rigid and his head raised high. His eyes seemed wild and his nostrils flared and quivered. Clive warned me not to approach him

Olive and Thunder

because the horse was frightened over his unaccustomed surroundings. He said he would have to win his trust before he would be able to ride him. And once Thunder is comfortable with Clive he will let others ride him.

Clive kept his distance but didn't seem to need words to communicate with him. I contented myself with currying Bess. She is always glad to see me.

I still remember the day six years ago when we bought Bess. Mother being in a delicate way expecting William, and Sister being ill with the grippe, Papa took me with him to the fair at the village. It seemed a most wonderful occasion, crowded with villagers and Papa's tenants, many of whom doffed their hats or bobbed curtsies in deference and affection.

There were many gymnastic contests. Grown men were competing climbing greased poles, but mostly sliding down the poles, it seemed. And then there were the sack races—the younger men competed in these.

A man was walking a tight wire high above the ground. I worried about him, but Papa reassured me that the very long pole he was using for balance made the feat safe.

There were stalls with hawkers selling tea, lemonade, ginger beer, pickled eels, smoked herrings, fruit tarts, even pineapples. Without Nanny or Mother along, I was allowed to eat all and everything I wanted. I couldn't stop eating the gaufers, so wonderfully gingery. I felt very grown up drinking a ginger beer, pretending it was a real beer like Papa's. I wanted to pet the bear, who was drinking his beer out of a bottle. But Papa warned me not to get close, as he was a very powerful animal.

A group of men were crowded around a pit, where I could hear dogs barking. Papa refused to let me go to the pit to see the dogs. He frowned and said he didn't approve of such cruel sports as dog fighting or cock fighting and would like to see laws passed against such practices. But he pointed out that it takes more than laws, it takes the backing of the people. A law was passed in 1835 against bear baiting, and yet he felt certain that the bear we had seen was being exhibited to let people know there was an illegal program going on in some clandestine place.

Papa did let me watch the pugilists. The loser had blood gushing from his nose and was knocked senseless and I wondered why Papa did not think this sport was cruel.

We visited the animal exhibition area to look at all the sheep, cattle, and horses. In that area I spotted the strangest-looking man, sitting on a low platform mounted on wheels. Though an exceedingly big man, and handsome of feature, his arms and legs were like those of an infant. I could not help but stare at such a strange creature. To my surprise, Papa seemed to know him and went over to speak to him.

When we left, Papa instructed me that it was wrong to stare at persons who are unfortunate. He asked me if I had noticed in Grandfather's library the painting of his championship pig. He explained that Mr. John Vine, for that was this deformed person's name, had once been on exhibit along with a bearded woman, a man who weighed in excess of twenty-eight stone, a two-headed calf, and other strange freaks of nature. Grandfather, having seen an oil painting Mr. Vine had painted, commissioned him to paint his prize sow. He was well pleased with the results and persuaded Mr. Vine he could make a living going to the fairs and painting the prize animals of which the owners were so proud.

I had frequently thought that the picture of Grandfather's Grand Champion pig did not look like a real pig because, though the pig was hugely fat, his legs and feet were so very tiny they looked as if they could not possibly support his weight. I think Mr. Vine wanted to show that a creature could be a champion even if his limbs had never grown.

The minute I saw Bess, with her big soft brown eyes, I fell in love with her. She was a colt, only recently weaned from her mother. Papa, being in an indulgent mood, bought her for me, and I'd never been so happy.

We led her home behind our carriage. The roads were rough, full of pot holes, and overindulgence proved to be my downfall. Papa had to stop the carriage, and he held my head as I lost the partakings of the day.

When Nanny saw that Bess had four white legs she said to me in a singsong voice:

One white leg, buy him
Two white legs, try him
Three white legs, deny him
Four white legs and a white nose,
Take off his bridle and throw him to the crows.

I was very hurt and resented Nanny for ridiculing my most precious possession. Papa said that she was only quoting an old country saying, that she really didn't mean it, and that, anyway, Bess didn't have a white nose.

In spite of my nausea it was one of the happiest days of my life. I had Bess and I had Papa to myself for a whole day.

Dear Diary,

This morning when Mr. Austin-Brown asked me to recite the words I learned this week, I had difficulty remembering the meanings of all the words. He instructed me to use my words in sentences with a personal meaning, and told me that he will bring me a copybook in which to record them so they can be reviewed. He advised, "If you get to know a word well enough, it will take on a personality and you will have an affection for it." I am eager to expand my vocabulary. If I close my eyes, I can still hear Grandfather's voice commenting on the unintelligible gibberish of a writer in his <u>Quarterly</u>. He complained that anyone so inarticulate and lacking in respect for language must care little for accuracy of thought or feeling, or, in the end, for truth itself.

I will put these in my copy book:

Sagacious	Grandfather was sagacious.
Sanguine	Papa is sanguine.
Punctilious	Mother is punctilious.
Stringent	Nanny is stringent.
Obese	Cook is obese.
Agile	Clive is agile.
Querulous	William is querulous.
Perspicacious	Mr. Austin-Brown is perspicacious and also perspicuous.

For my own amusement, I made the sentence about Mr. Austin-Brown, but I would not want him to see it. I'll not put it in the copybook.

I now appreciate Mr. Austin-Brown's gift of a dictionary. I'm certain that I will find it useful all my life.

I requested of Mr. Austin-Brown a copy of the poem he had given me on my birthday. His face flushed, and for once he seemed tongue-tied. Finally he responded, "Better yet, I'll write another poem—not just dedicated to you, but about you this time."

Today Monsieur Fleury, the dancing master, accompanied by his pianist, came to give Mother and Papa lessons as well as me. Even William was invited to watch. Mother and Papa are brushing up on the reels and quadrilles they learned when they were young. Mother says dancing is important to acquire graceful movement and proper carriage. This is one instruction for which I am eager because I've always loved to dance. Even before I learned the steps I would twirl and dance whenever I heard music. I wish I could hear music whenever I wished. The pianist played the most beautiful pieces called waltzes. Our instructor says we must learn to waltz, as Queen Victoria and Prince Albert are very fond of it. Ever since they danced it when they were engaged, all the best people are having tea dances. With that he took Mother and twirled her around the room. Papa was scowling and protested that this was too much exertion for anyone of a frail constitution. I

think he disliked it that Monsieur Fleury had his arm around Mother's waist.

When I watch the dancing master I feel like laughing. The droll little man waves his hands around for gesticulation, interjecting French words. He ever so delicately points his very small feet clad in ballet slippers, and his frilly jabot bounces as he dances. Papa executes the steps with lightness of foot and fine flow, in spite of his muscular build. He seems to enjoy dancing even more than Mother.

William became bored and wanted to return to the nursery and play with his wooden soldiers. I found every minute fascinating, and I could have danced without fatigue all the afternoon.

Monsieur Fleury told Mother and Papa that the best people now engage in tableaux vivants, in which the participants dress to represent a painting or famous historical moment. He said it was great fun when Lord Langthorp, who has a luxuriant mustache, donned a veil and gown and played a seductive woman.

I asked Mother and Papa who the best people were. Mother responded that surely the three hundred titled families listed in Debrett's would be the best, as only those of legitimate birth are included. Papa thought a moment and said that he knew some scoundrels among them and he certainly couldn't call them the best people, legitimate or not. On the other hand, some people think they can purchase social respectability just as they can an estate. And some think that a proper accent and dress is sufficient for admission to gentility.

At that, Mother chimed in, "A mule dressed in a frock coat is still a mule."

Papa continued that, for him, the best people are those of high character, who show consideration for others, and who engage in activities for the betterment of mankind. And, of course, they need to be fond of manly sports, he added, and laughed his jovial chuckle.

All evening long the tunes danced in my head, and I danced around the bedchamber with a broomstick for a partner. It would be much more enjoyable with a real partner. I don't understand why Mr. Austin-Brown was not invited to the instruction.

I've always liked to sleep with the window open. The fresh air I find exhilarating. When I opened the window I heard Mother playing the pianoforte and singing. Occasionally, Papa joined in. It makes me happy to hear them. Their two voices blend so beautifully together. I wished I could be there singing with them, but I would not want to ruin their harmony with my lack of voice.

Dear Diary,

Our geography and history lessons today were about China. We learned that England started trading with China way back in Great-grandfather's day, and then China closed the country to foreigners and established the Kongs, the trading houses in the port now called Hong Kong.

Mother invited William and me to take tea in the drawing room with Papa and her and Cousin Hubert. Mother serves cakes and sweetmeats with our tea, like her Mother did and her Grandmother before her. Anna, Duchess of Bedford, invited her Grandmother to take tea at Belvoir Castle and, as the Duchess was a portly lady with a hearty appetite, she had need of sustenance before her customary late dinner. Mother says that it soon became the fashionable custom among the best people. I love it when I am invited.

As we passed through the dining room I paused to look at the wallpaper. Though I'd seen it all my life I had new interest after our lesson about China. Grandfather once told me it was a gift from Emperor Ch'ien-lung in 1780 to Great-grandfather, who built our house. It is a scene of trees with strange foliage, a pagoda with a pointed roof, and Chinese people in strange-looking clothes with parasols, and happy-faced Chinese children playing with birds. There is even a plump little Chinese boy with a topknot, riding a huge turtle. I wish we had birds in England that children could play with. I think

William would be afraid to ride a turtle. Grandfather told me that Great-grandfather admired the pagoda so much he had Mr. Capability Brown, the landscape architect, design a pagoda in our park. He had our cabinetmaker make the chairs with the lattice fretwork backs, taking the design from a detail of a fence in the wallpaper. William pulled up one of the chairs to the table and climbed on it to see if there were sweetmeats in the cups of the silver epergne in the center of the table. Grandfather had his goldsmith fashion it like a pagoda and presented it to Mother and Papa on the occasion of their wedding. I reprimanded William for scratching the table with his shoes.

Nanny always coaches me to observe Mother carefully as she serves tea so that I can do it properly when I have my own household. When the footman Egbert brought in the hot water and the tea service Mother unlocked the tea caddy with the key she keeps on her chatelaine along with her scissors and other important household instruments. She mixed the tea leaves in the little bowl in the caddy with the special silver measuring spoon. Mother prefers the green teas from China. She says she looked forward to the new teas from India when they were first imported ten years ago, but she finds them unattractively black and too burnt and harsh for her taste. Her hands are so slender and graceful. She never spills a drop when she pours the tea through the tea strainer into the cup. I'll never be able to do it as well as she does.

She handles the sugar nips with graceful ease. Cousin Hubert and Papa requested three lumps. William also. I asked for two lumps. Mother said nothing but put only one lump in her cup and mine.

Mother complains about my sweet tooth. I've heard her tell her guests the story of how clever her little dog once was. She found him barking one day at something no one could see. She feared it was our ghost, but upon investigation, she found that what had attracted his interest was me, hidden under the draped table, clutching the sugar bowl with a mouth full of sugar lumps. I wish she would stop telling that story. It was ever so long ago. I was much younger than William is today.

When William was offered the sugar castor to sprinkle his strawberries, he shook it so vigorously that powdered sugar spilled all over Mother's new Aubusson rug. Since William is Mother's pride and pleasure, she frowned but she didn't say anything.

Cousin Hubert complimented the beautiful china cups. I commented that since he called them china cups they must have come from China. Papa explained that the reason we call them china is that before we English learned to make porcelain, all our fine cups came from China. Mother explained that the design on them is a Phoenix, which according to legend is a bird that rose from its own ashes and thus is a symbol of hope. It has such long feathers that a child couldn't <u>hope</u> to play with it, but then it's not a real bird anyway.

While we were conversing, William had taken from the tea table the silver sugar container Grandfather's goldsmith had fashioned in the shape of a tortoise, and was playing with it on the floor. When Papa reprimanded him and instructed him to return the container to the tea tray, he set up a howl of protest. Papa had Egbert escort him back to the nursery and I felt glad. Nanny had warned him that children should be seen and not heard.

Now that I'm grown I like tea, but William prefers the cocoa, with lots of hot milk, that we are served in the nursery. Even better than the tea are the biscuits and meat sandwiches. Papa once explained that we call them sandwiches because the Earl of Sandwich enjoyed taking his meal in that fashion so that he could stay at the gaming-table around the clock without interruption. As for the biscuits, I would have liked to take the whole biscuit barrel full. I slipped one in my pocket for later enjoyment. I hope that's not stealing.

Dear Diary,

Mother is feeling poorly. She has a headache today. We must all be very quiet, even William. This is hard for William. He always talks loudly because that is the only way Nanny can hear him. Papa tiptoes around looking very concerned. When she is suffering so, only Ainslie is allowed to remain in her chambers. On occasion when it is too severe, Papa administers to her twelve drops of laudanum, which he procures from the apothecarist. She remains in her dressing gown, sends for a cup of feverfew tea, closes the blinds, and lies on her daybed, her <u>lit du repose</u>, with slices of cucumber on her eyes and on her face her own special lotion of rose water and tincture of mallow leaves and a little honey.

Everyone admires Mother's beautiful complexion. Her fragile skin shines like moonlight and is almost as translucent. I

Ainslie on his new pillow

guess that is why Papa calls her "Moonbeam." Papa shows that he likes you by calling you nicknames. He calls Nanny "Nan Nan" because when he was little she was his Nanny. He calls William "Soldier" unless he's disciplining him, and then he calls him William. He called his sister Emma, who died on the island of Virgin Gorda in the West Indies, "Swan," because she had a beautiful long neck. Dearest Sister Amy he called "Little Angel" because no one ever had to reprimand her. Mrs. Potts is always just "Cook" to Papa but she doesn't mind. I asked him once why he called me Cygnet. He just hugged me and said, "One day you will understand." I thought I saw a tear in his eye.

I'm wondering what really causes headaches. Some people say that God is punishing us, but I don't think that is it at all. What could Mother have done that she needs to be punished so? I think if we knew why we had them we could learn how to fix them.

Even though William was over in the nursery, he could be heard beating his drum. So I took him down to the gallery to keep his rumpus from disturbing Mother.

There are four white marble statues on pedestals in front of the windows. When I was younger I once stared at them so long that they seemed to come alive. I thought they were wearing sheets, which convinced me that they were ghosts. Papa laughed and explained that they are wearing togas, and that they are not ancestors at all but busts of him and three of his friends. When he was a young man and on his Grand Tour of Europe he commissioned the busts in Rome from an American sculptor, Mr. Hiram Powers. Most of the ancient statues had already been purchased by Grandfather's generation long before Papa went there. I remember that Papa commented, "Leave it to an American to think of re-creating antique statues." I hope I get to meet an American some day.

There is a picture of Grandfather in the portrait gallery dressed in the robes he wore when he served in Parliament. The picture does not look like I remember him, but of course he was much younger then. I explained to William that many of the men in the paintings were our ancestors. William thought some of the men were women, their hair was so long. I had to explain they were wearing wigs, and that men like barristers and judges still do the same.

My favourite picture is one of a family group just like my family. I like it because they look as if they are happy. It's a mother and father and three children. The mother is holding the plump little boy, who looks much like William, in her lap. The oldest girl is playing with a King Charles spaniel just like Mother's Ainslie. Although the father does not have sideburns like Papa, he has chestnut-coloured hair and a Roman nose like Papa's. He is holding hands with the middle girl, who looks so much like Sister. Dearest Sister had such beautiful naturally curly hair. I wrap my hair in rags at night, but by midday my curls are dolefully collapsed. Not one of the family in the painting looks like me at all.

I wonder why people sometimes query where I got my blond hair and blue eyes and who it is I favour. Papa always answers God makes everyone different and jokes that he'd feel sorry for me if I looked like him. I think his features are most handsome and he just says that in consideration of my plainness.

I remember when Dearest Sister was sick. With her rosy cheeks, she appeared so healthy I never realized the severity of her illness. Papa believes in the efficacy of sunshine, fresh air, and daily exercise and thought saline immersion might help her, so he wanted to take her to the seashore. Nanny decided her illness was caused by the damp night air in our vale. She believes we should never open a window in our bedchamber. Mother prepared red clover tea and tonics with herbs and fed them to her from her posset cup when she became too weak to sit up. The doctor prescribed draughts, and when they didn't help tried bleeding with leeches. Cousin Hubert came and prayed with the family both morning and evening. Mrs. Potts said the child needed ass's milk and Papa bought not only a jenny but also a jack, whose braying awakened Nanny even in spite of her deafness.

But Dearest Sister coughed and coughed until she was too weak to cough any more.

I asked Papa why God let her die. He said, "Life is only a

breath when we think of eternity." Cousin Hubert said, "We will be with her in Heaven, which will be forever." In my prayer tonight I will remember to thank God that I had her as long as I did, and to promise Him that I will try to be good so I can be with her again in Heaven.

Dear Diary,

Papa instructed Mr. Austin-Brown to shorten my lesson so that I could ride with him on his rounds of the estate today. I was tickled pink. He rode on Thunder and I was on Bess. Clive already has Thunder calmed, and Papa rode him without difficulty. Of course, Papa is an excellent horseman with good hands. Though Thunder had settled down and Papa kept him reined in, Bess couldn't keep up with Thunder's long sweeping thoroughbred strides. I wished for a faster horse and told Papa I thought we should give Bess to William. I reminded him that William is of sufficient age to ride her now. Bess is such a sweet little English mare, gentle by nature with pleasant manners, and never kicks or bucks. Besides, she is sure-footed, never stumbles, and, as she is but fourteen hands high, she is not a threat for a fall.

When we rode by Tenant Swinert's home, Papa stopped to reprove him for his littered enclosure. His wife was sitting on an upturned log out in the sunlight so that she could better see to spin. The baby started crying, so with one foot she rocked the cradle by her side. Her unkempt hair kept falling over her eyes. One of her little girls was braiding straw with which to make hats and another was attaching pearl buttons, made from seashells, to cards.

Papa made converse with Mrs. Swinert, telling her that soon it would not be necessary to card and spin the wool, as

Bess

that will all be done by a machine powered by a steam engine and cloth will be able to be bought at a reasonable price. Papa had meant this as good news, but the poor woman looked distressed. "But how will I feed my children then?" she asked.

At that moment a child with grimy bare feet ran from the door of the cottage and we heard the loud voice of a man cursing. He appeared at the door, his hair disheveled, his face blotched and florid, and he was staggering as he walked. Papa informed Tenant Swinert that the government has established schools in each town, and though the government did not make it compulsory, it would be beneficial to his children to send them. His answer was almost incoherent, but the sense of it was a boast that his children were earning good wages and didn't need schooling. Papa forgot to speak to him about the litter.

As we rode away I spoke to Papa of my disappointment that we did not see the Swinerts' son Lettuce. He was such a nice boy and used to join Dearest Sister and me when we played house in the hollow tree in the oak copse near their cottage. He would push me in the rope swing so high my feet almost touched the sky. He made a ball by wrapping wool around a rock and sewing it in an old sock. With Lettuce all of our games were more enjoyable.

Papa explained that Lettuce and his brother both work making pottery in the village. He shook his head and said, "Yes, they walk four miles to the village, work twelve hours at a pot house, and have no future!" He explained that there is insufficient work in agriculture for the increase in population today and other opportunities for employment must be developed or our country will face a disaster.

When we returned home I heard Papa tell Mother, "If that man would leave the gin bottle alone, he could make a decent living for his family. I know he poaches a grouse or a hare regularly and even a deer on occasion. I should have him transported to Australia, but I just look the other way because the family is sickly enough without them starving. I should dismiss the man, but what would become of those children?

I hate the thought of them being in the workhouse. If the man was not so worthless he could at least grow a garden for his family. He let the plants die which I instructed Thomas to take to him. And I had even sent him a watering can."

The emaciated mother has a baby almost every year. Mother sends food, and when Mrs. Swinert is sick Mother takes medicines to her, but she won't allow me to accompany her. When the last baby was born the mother's milk was insufficient. Mother took her fennel seeds from her herb garden for tea, and it must have helped, for the baby lived.

Thunder seems a gentle horse now. He even let me pat him and stroke his forehead. Clive may not be agile with words but he is exceedingly good with horses. I'm certain Papa will allow me to ride Thunder very soon.

Dear Diary,

On our way to services this morning we stopped at the church graveyard as usual. I wanted to place a bouquet on Dear Sister's grave. Ainslie jumped from Mother's arms and raced around the tombstones until Tenant Godwin's son captured him and returned him to Mother.

Our family plot is getting crowded; it's been so many years since Great-great-grandfather was buried there in 1782. There is the grave of Papa's Great-uncle George, who was killed in a duel, in an affair of honour. On his tombstone it reads,

> *How blest is our brother bereft*
> *Of all that could burden his mind.*
> *How easy the soul that has left*
> *This worrisome body behind.*

The gravestone of Great-uncle John, Grandfather's younger brother who was killed in the Battle of Waterloo, has the insignia of the Royal Cavalry. He must have been a hero, because Grandfather told me that salvos were fired over his grave at the funeral. Grandfather's grave is there next to the grandmother I never knew. Papa never knew her either because she died in childbed when he was born. Papa's brother Henry, who died a very young man when his gun backfired while he was shooting grouse, is buried next to Papa's sister Emma Amelia, who died in the West Indies. Her fiancé had been sent there to assist the Captain General in seeing that there was a peaceful transition in the freeing of the slaves. She had gone there to be married, only to find that he had died of the yellow fever before her ship reached shore. She died, they said, of a broken heart. Papa made the trip there to bring her body home. On the return voyage his ship encountered a terrible storm which I think is called a hurricane. He had great fear that the ship would sink. That was a long time ago when I was only a tiny baby. I hope there will still be room for me in the churchyard when I die.

The grass has covered Dearest Sister's grave, but the white marble angel with outspread arms guarding over her is clear of moss, unlike the other gravestones. When I read the words carved under her name tears came to my eyes.

Our Angel on Earth Is Now an Angel in Heaven.

Sister radiated from within with love, purity, and gentleness. She never lost her temper like I do. No wonder Papa used to call her "Little Angel." She sometimes had a faraway look in her eyes, as if she could see something that I could never see.

Papa was holding my hand and he squeezed it saying, "Don't cry, Little Cygnet, your sister is in a better place, where there is no strife and discord, only peace and love." I guess it was wrong of me to wish she was still alive, but I do because I never told her that I loved her. I didn't know how much until she was gone. I was sorry I had ever teased her and called her "Miss Goody Two Shoes."

William squirms around even more than Mother's dog, Ainslie. Mother explained that it is permissible to take Ainslie to church because King Charles loved his Cavalier spaniels so much he decreed that though dogs are not permitted to attend services, his breed of dog would henceforth be an exception.

Today Cousin Hubert was talking about the Holy Ghost. I thought of our ghost in Primrose Hall. More than once I asked about the ghost, but no one wanted to talk about it. Finally, I tricked Crawford into telling me. I knew that if anyone knew he would, because he has been in service to our family all his life, as his father was before him.

The ghost is Great-grandfather's sister. I never learned her name because her grave is not in the church graveyard as she could not be buried in consecrated ground. The man she was to marry cancelled the wedding when he discovered she was with child, which, of course, was such a shameful condition that she had despondent fits and developed a fever in her brain. Her parents would never send her to a terrible place like Bedlam, so she was confined to her room on the top floor. One day she flung herself from the window. Crawford says he can't blame her fiancé and that she is paying for her sin by having to remain in this world as a ghost.

Crawford says that if we had spiral chimneys the ghost could have escaped. Nanny says the ghost never comes to the nursery wing because it's too new. Mrs. Potts says if the ghost came into her kitchen she'd chase it out with her rolling pin. The chambermaid won't even talk about ghosts. The subject frightens her so that she refuses to clean in that bedroom. No guest is ever housed there, no matter how many guests we have, because the ghost visits at night.

The ghost does not scare Papa at all. I guess that's because she is an ancestor of his. Of course that makes her a relative of mine, too, so I shouldn't be afraid either.

William asserted that it was scary to think of Jesus as a ghost, but I assured him that He's a very good ghost. I'd ask Cousin Hubert to explain to William, but I don't think he would understand his answers. Sometimes they seem to be just words. Cousin Hubert likes words, lots of words. Papa says Cousin Hubert likes unusual words because he thinks that they lend an air of distinction to his conversation. Nanny says Cousin Hubert is pompous as well as pious.

My new words for my copybook today were easy to find in my dictionary because they both started with a p. Pompous and pious. And I don't have to think of sentences for them because Nanny did that for me. But I don't think of Cousin Hubert as pompous—loquacious, garrulous, or verbose perhaps, but not pompous.

I told Nanny I have decided to memorize every word in my dictionary. Crotchety Nanny had to say, "I think you are biting off more than you can chew."

Dear Diary,

During lessons Mother sent Abigail to tell Mr. Austin-Brown to release me early, as her dressmaker, Mrs. Taylor, was here to make us new gowns for a party Mother and Papa are planning during the fall hunt. This is the first time I will be allowed to attend the party. I am so excited to think I will be going. Mother has cautioned me that I must look demure, not speak unless spoken to, and even then answer only yes or no.

Dearest Sister and I used to tiptoe to the upstairs hall and peek between the banisters to watch the beautifully gowned ladies below. We could hear the music and we would dance in our bare feet until Nanny discovered us and made us go to bed.

Mother allowed me to look through the beautiful materials in her fabric chest: Indian chintz, block printed calico and fustian for indoor wear, cambric, serge for everyday of course, but damasks, pekin silk, taffetas, brocades, and levantines for special occasions. Many came from faraway places like China or India, or lands close by like Ireland and France. I ran my hand over them because I love feeling their differentness—some all smooth and soft, and others crisp or rustly. Mother sent me to her washbasin to wash my hands, even though her warm water had cooled.

Mother has an extensive collection of buttons. She procures some on every journey as well as from the button peddler who comes by the Hall. When I was little, Dearest Sister

Mrs. Taylor

and I considered it a treat to play with them. We would sort them and arrange them in rows, making pictures. My favourites were those with birds and Sister's were those with flowers.

I still remember a day, years ago now, when we were playing with the buttons. I was replacing them in their box, and I noticed that one of them was missing. William was a baby, and had been crawling on the floor nearby. Mother feared that William had swallowed the button and admonished me sharply for putting the buttons where he could reach them. I picked him up by his heels and pounded him on the back. Great bawling came from his mouth but no button. Very upset, Mother scolded me sharply for hurting him. I then noticed one of his fists was clinched and I pried it open. There was the button. Mother was so relieved she couldn't stop hugging and kissing him. She forgot to apologize to me for losing her temper.

This morning Mother had laid out her old dresses, which had been in her storage chest so long that they smelled of naphtha. She needs many new dresses, as she has been in mourning crepe for a long time for Dearest Sister, and before that for Grandfather. Mrs. Taylor brought her Godey pattern book with the latest French designs. She lamented that the styles had changed little for the last two years because of the political unrest in Paris.

Papa complained that the French seem to want people not

to be able to tell the women from the men. They now have women wearing paletots, and he wishes women would stay with shawls and cloaks. With a twinkle in his eye Papa teased that bonnets have become the only way you can tell it's a woman and then you can't see their faces, which is a deprivation. Mother says I'm not old enough to wear a bonnet. I wonder if I will be next year.

Mrs. Taylor urged that, along with a ball gown, Mother needed a carriage dress, a walking dress, a tea gown, and a morning dress. But these will have to be made later in the year, for it requires much time to make even one dress. For the carriage dress Mother selected a dress of pekin with satin stripes, green and rose in colour. The flounces on the skirt are each to be edged with green silk fringe, beaded with two rows of green velvet. The tight sleeves will be finished with turn-up cuffs. Mrs. Taylor assured her that her cabriolet bonnet of pink cherry velvet, freshened with a trim of white lace and a white violette attached to the edge, would look perfect with the dress. She recommended yellow kid gloves, which I felt to be the wrong colour.

Mother chose a brown walking gown, the pardessus of the paletot form, with deep rows of quilting. She also ordered down-filled undergarments, which should provide a sufficient degree of warmth for the promenade. This is important, as Mother tends to chill very easily. Though Mrs. Taylor recommended slate-coloured kid gloves, I think the yellow ones will go quite well with this costume.

For Papa, Mother ordered a nightshirt and a brocaded robe with a silk muffler. He said he will visit his tailor on his next trip to London. I am so excited to think that I will probably get to go on the next visit to London.

For William, Mother chose a costume consisting of a paletot of grey cloth edged with darker grey soutache embroidery, his black trousers to be gathered on a band at the waist, black leather shoes and gaiters of chamois leather from the Alps. To top it all, a black felt hat with a cord finished with two tassels instead of a band. I could but think that William won't keep the hat on his head and it will soon be lost.

As a special treat for William, Mother suggested that Mrs. Taylor make a grenadier's cap from her old fur muff. I'm sure William will never lose it. Mother also asked Mrs. Taylor to make a cushion for Ainslie out of her old paisley shawl. She justified her indulgence for her pet by pointing out that it is not a real Kashmir, as this one was made in Scotland, not India.

Mother's ball gown itself is to be the latest model. Mrs. Taylor says it is modeled from one worn by a cousin of Prince Albert, a princess of Saxe-Coburg. The bodice is drawn into a long point, the neckline finished with a wide band of pleated fabric like picture frame molding, all in the most delicious strawberry-coloured satin.

I was not given the privilege of selecting a pattern, because Mother had already chosen a style. It is so old-fashioned Grandmother might have worn it when she was a child! I think Mother would like to have me in pantalets! Mother always dressed Sister and me as if we were twins. As I am eleven months older, I resented being dressed like a baby. Now if I could only have Dearest Sister back I would not mind at all. I immediately loved the robin's-egg blue satin for my dress, but Mother reminded me that dress not only provides a clue to character but also affects the personality, and my selection was not the proper fabric for a girl my age. And besides, she has bought a piece of white embroidered muslin especially for me. And that was that. Sometimes I think that Mother does not want me to grow up. When Mrs. Taylor saw the tears of disappointment in my eyes she suggested that we trim my dress with rosettes made of blue riband, and she even showed me how to make the rosettes. I attached the sample rosette in my hair, and tilted the cheval looking glass so that I could see it from all sides. I was so happy visualizing how grown-up I would look at the party.

I spent the afternoon practicing on a length of old riband. But I never could make my rosettes as pretty as Mrs. Taylor did, and I finally burst into tears. Nanny chided me: "Perhaps you're not meant to wear rosettes in your hair! It's not important." When I protested, she continued, "Remember, young lady, pretty is as pretty does. Purity of manners, fine sensibility,

Mother and William in their promenade attire

chastity, modesty, sweetness of nature, temper meek—that's what's important." She made me promise to record this list in my journal. I was so thankful that she didn't say to write it a hundred times.

Even with the help of her assistant seamstress it takes Mrs. Taylor ever so long to make just one dress. Her perfect stitches are so tiny and fine. I told Papa it would be wonderful if there was a machine to make the stitches for her. If a machine can be made that will pull a big train, surely one could be invented to pull the thread through the cloth.

Dear Diary,

Nanny and I were in front of the hall enjoying the sunshine, watching William trying to catch a frog in the bed of primroses surrounding the fountain, when a horseman arrived with letters for Papa.

On our way to deliver Papa's correspondence we encountered Ainslie in the back hall eating out of his crystal feeding dish. And here came Goliath growling in his deep guttural voice.

William shrank back in fear.

As I anticipated, the ever-hungry Goliath only wanted to partake of Ainslie's meal. As he neared Ainslie, the little dog turned and growled back at him. To my amusement Goliath backed away, retreating meekly to his spot in the dog kennel cupboard. I laughed and pointed out to William that Goliath is an old softie and not one to be feared. Nanny had to add, "You see, William, his bark is worse than his bite."

Even though it is the day for the tenants to pay their rent, Papa always takes time to talk to Nanny and tell her how pretty she is looking. Nanny and William proceeded upstairs to deliver a letter for Mother but I stayed to talk with Papa. When the first tenant arrived I retired to the window bench with my book. I hoped Papa would let me stay, as I had not seen some of the families since they had come to pay their respects when Grandfather died. That day it seemed as if the whole countryside came. They stood patiently in line, and even the children were silent as they filed past the open casket. I didn't want to look at Grandfather in his casket. I wanted only to remember his kind eyes and gentle countenance. When I had to view his body I kept my eyes shut.

All the tenants treat Papa with great respect. I know they must admire him, because he gives counsel to them on personal concerns as well as their business affairs. After Papa paid Farmer Godwin for his share of the crops, Farmer Godwin said, "Your pardon, Sir, I want to say how happy and satisfied I and my family are with our life here on the estate. We have a roof over our heads, plenty of food to eat, and the satisfaction of seeing and enjoying the fruit of our labour."

After he departed Papa explained to me that this man had once been in debtors' prison. He reflected, "Sometimes we have to have been without to appreciate what we have. Debt can be a poor substitute for what it purchases. Remember, Cygnet, it's important to value what you have instead of concentrating on what you don't."

Papa asked each tenant not only about his crops or animals but also about his wife and children. There are many children I did not even know existed. He urged each one to send their children to the school the government has established in our village, and offered to pay half of the fees if they will pay the other half, as the charge is only a few pence.

Since the charge is indeed modest I asked Papa why he did

not pay the full tuition. He explained that every decent man wants to provide for his family and we must not destroy his dignity. Besides, education would be considered of no value if it cost nothing.

Each tenant has a triangular-shaped drawer in the circular rent table into which Papa places his payment after making an entry into the record book. In some cases where Papa marketed that farmer's produce he paid the tenant. The very last person to arrive was Farmer Swinert. He had bathed and shaved and looked nothing like he did the day Papa and I rode by his cottage. He had only a small portion of his rent money. I could tell Papa was upset and very angry about this, as the vein in his forehead throbbed and he pursed his lips. But he did not raise his voice; instead in a very level tone, he declared that Farmer Swinert was going to have to mend his ways. He offered, as to the others, to pay half the tuition for his children's education, which was very generous, as there are so very many Swinerts. He asked Tenant Swinert about his children. They have such strange names: Ham, Feather, Despair, Uz, and Lettuce. The other names are so odd I can't remember them. I have never known anyone else who didn't have a proper Christian name. I have never seen them at services in church. Unlike some of the other landowners, Papa does not require his tenants to pay a fine if they do not attend church. He says that faith and love cannot be legislated.

When Papa opened Tenant Swinert's drawer, out jumped a

big frog right in his face. Startled, Papa reared backwards, upsetting his chair. His head hit the floor with a very loud thud. Farmer Swinert burst out laughing, his fleshy jowls puffing in and out like a bullfrog himself. Papa lay there stunned. I glared at Farmer Swinert as I rushed to Papa. Though he had received a severe blow he had not lost consciousness. Farmer Swinert quit laughing, but stood there like the dullard he is.

"Cygnet," Papa said weakly, "are you the culprit who played that prank on me?"

"Oh, Papa, you know I wouldn't do anything to hurt you," I replied. I started to tell Papa who the culprit was, but he interrupted me.

"Never mind, love, it was a good trick and with no harm meant, I'm sure."

If I had placed the frog there I would have meant harm, but never to Papa; rather to that odious Mr. Swinert.

I thanked God that I have my wonderful Papa and Mother, who are kind and never yell at me.

William finds a frog

Dear Diary,

Mother and Papa left for the London house today. I hugged and kissed Papa and beseeched permission to go. I could have wept if I had allowed myself. It seems there is always some reason I cannot go to the city. Papa said that they would not be gone long but had to go because he had important commerce with some nabobs from India. Besides I have my lessons and they are important. He promised that he and Mother would send many letters, even though the penny post does not come so deep in the country as Primrose Hall. I resent being left at home with that pesty William.

Papa told me that any day now a young woman named Bridget would be coming from Ireland because of the famine there. He has engaged her as a chambermaid, and as she is not much older than I am, he would like me to show her around the estate and help make her feel more comfortable. Crawford will direct her as to her duties, of course. I felt proud that Papa entrusted me with that responsibility.

As they left he winked at Mother and said, "Hurry up, love. The early bird catches the worm."

She replied, "Remember, dear, a bird in the hand is worth two in the bush!"

"Well," he replied, "this time I hope to kill two birds with one stone."

"Just remember," she continued, "birds of a feather flock together."

Papa said, "All right, Moonbeam, you win!"

Mother retorted, "You started it with your Nannyism." Then they laughed together. Their jocular exchange allayed my despondent mood.

The carriage was so laden with bandboxes, bonnet boxes, and trunks, there was little room for the footman. Papa's lap desk was tucked under the seat. Ainslie was yapping at the window as the carriage clattered off. Papa stuck his head out the window to wave good-bye and knocked his top hat off. Egbert jumped down off the back to retrieve it and winked good-bye to me. He had confided to me that he was going to seek employment in the city now that his twelve months are near to end. He said that Primrose Hall is too much in the country for his taste, for he's not so old that he is not one for a bit of life, himself. I was sad to see him leave, for he could spin a droll yarn.

It was a beautiful sunshiny day. Nanny said that even though the currants have finished, there should be the wild raspberries, and if I picked a bucketful Cook might save enough from her raspberry jam to make the pudding she makes every summer using bread and berries. As I left the house, Nanny called, "If the raspberries are finished, check the gooseberry shrubs and I'll ask her to make a gooseberry fool. But mind the briers, brambles, and thorns."

As I was walking through the park down to the wild raspberry bushes, I spied two saucy robin redbreasts hopping around pulling worms up out of the grass. Remembering what Mother had said, I hoped the two birds had not eaten all the berries before I could harvest them. I was lucky. The limbs of the bushes were heavy with berries. Before the birds got there my basket was full. The scent of the ripe fruit warmed by the sun filled my nostrils, tempting me to eat a few on my way back to the kitchen. Mrs. Potts usually won't let me stay in the kitchen, but she was in a good mood today because I had brought her the raspberries. So she let me watch her make the pudding and even suggested that I copy the receipt, telling me that if I liked the pudding that well I needed the receipt for the day when I have my own house and my own cook. Mrs. Potts is so old she will be dead before that day. And even if she were still cooking she would stay here in this place, which will one day belong to my brother, of course.

Mrs. Potts must have the most wonderful work in the whole world. All those delicious smells and wonderful things to eat. And she has Liz to help her in the scullery. I'd be so happy if I could be a cook when I grow up. I'd make biscuits and puddings every day.

When I went back to the nursery and told Nanny that I had helped make the pudding so it was sure to be good, she chastised me. "Don't boast, child," she said. "If you toot your own horn you won't get tooted. And stop your pouting— would you rather be ruined by praise than saved by criticism?"

I noticed that she and William ate every bite, so I felt proud. Nanny must have known what I was thinking, for she said, "The proof of the pudding is in the eating." That made me feel happy. Happiness is cooking a good dish, and even better, eating it!

I've been thinking that Mother and Papa were not talking about birds at all this morning.

MRS. POTTS'S SUMMER PUDDING

Sugar well the available fruit with Lisbon sugar. Powdered sugar may be used, but the Lisbon sugar imparts a more mellowed flavour. Fill a deep tart dish with alternate layers of the fruit and very thin slices of the crumb of a light stale loaf released from its crust; let the upper layer be of fruit, and it should be of a dry kind. Sprinkle over it a dessertspoonful of water, a little lemon juice; raspberries, currants, and cherries will not require this. Be certain to release the cherries from their stones and stalks. Send the pudding to a somewhat brisk but not fierce oven to be baked for a very brief time. If you wish to serve cold, send to the cool-house and place a heavy object, such as an iron, on top to release the juices into the bread. If of insufficient sweetness, strew with sugar sifted through a hair sieve.

Dear Diary,

It is raining today. To entertain William I took him to Grand-father's library to look at his collections and curiosities. William's favourites are the fossil collection, the crocodile mummy from Egypt, and the drawers upon drawers of care-fully preserved insects. My favourite collections are the shells and the bird eggs, some so tiny and some speckled and some beautiful colours. There is even an ostrich egg. Grandfather had the goldsmith mount it with a silver bird foot for the stand.

I think Grandfather's favourite was the collection of boxes he brought back as souvenirs from his journeys. Papa also brought him several from his travels. Some have scenes of for-eign cities, some are fabricated of material indigenous to the site where they were purchased, and some commemorate an event, such as his box celebrating Her Royal Highness's coro-nation. A unique one is of horn with metal fittings, topped with a tiny medallion that bears the profile of Napoleon. It was Grandfather's custom to pick up a box and recall the occasion and locale of the purchase. Even though he was no longer able to travel, he said that without setting a foot outside his library he could be transported upon the most wonderful journeys. With one box he could be in Italy, with the very next in India. He said he imagines an exploration all the better because it was without danger or discomfort. As Grandfather often reflected, in his gentle voice, "Remember, Cygnet, that the best companion of all is one's own mind."

Grandfather spent almost all of his days in his study, for he had experienced great difficulty walking ever since the day his horse failed to clear a stream and his leg was crushed in the fall. He used to spend hours reading the Quarterly or attending to his correspondence, especially with his literary friends Mr. Wordsworth and Mr. Thackeray. One day he told me about a letter he once received from Mr. Coleridge. He wrote that he had composed a whole poem in a dream and upon awakening had written several lines when a person from Porlock interrupted him. Then he couldn't remember the rest of the poem. He named it "Kubla Khan," and Grandfather said that it has since become famous.

I wish I would dream poems instead of my terrible nightmare. Cousin Hubert says God can speak to us through our dreams. I try and try to think what His message is in my terrible nightmare. But sometimes I do dream beautiful colourful pictures. I wonder if God is telling me to appreciate His world. I wonder if Mr. Austin-Brown dreams his poems.

I love Grandfather's astronomical globe. One day he showed me the different constellations. When he pointed out Cygnus he told me the Greek myth about Leander, who was turned into a swan. For some strange reason Grandfather had tears in his eyes, and he drew me close to him and hugged me and called me his Little Cygnet.

Before I could read well he read me many interesting stories but that was before his eyesight failed. Even though he ate flowers of the rosemary plant to clear his sight, finally he could no longer see to read, even with his spectacles.

After that I spent many hours every day, reading to him. Sometimes I thought that he had memorized his books, because if I skipped a paragraph he would correct me. Some books he had read many times. He said that it was like a fresh encounter with an old friend. I don't like to read the same book twice. There are too many waiting on the shelf for me.

His shelves are lined with books furnished with interesting and exciting personages, but I'll never be able to read all of them because many are in Greek or Latin. He once waved his hand and said, "See what an inexhaustible reservoir—what a Bank of England to draw upon for profitable thought—there is before you. Now that age has come and stolen my pleasure, my books are a consolation. Little Cygnet, store your mind with the treasure of Knowledge! Let yourself be led into mental encounters. You can have a conversation with a book that can be an enlightening adventure. It can point out your potential—and your peril."

Grandfather said that he had always taken delight in the constant society of books, and he especially loved poetry. When I would read the poetry he loved and a Greek or Roman god was mentioned, he would pull out the drawers of the little mahogany chest containing the gilt-edged intaglios he had purchased in Rome when he was a youth on his Grand Tour of Europe. He'd select the ones with the images of the particular gods referred to, and then relate the myth. One day I commented that there are so many gods, and they have such adventures, that it was no wonder the poets so frequently refer to them. Grandfather smiled and quipped, "Maybe they just like to show that they've studied the classics." When I told him Cousin Hubert declared them but heathen mythology, Grandfather reflected a moment and then said, "Mythology must not replace our God the Father, the Son, and the Holy Spirit. Yet mythology stimulates the imagination and gives understanding of the human condition. More than that, myths can be looked to for things that give meaning to life. From the classics, we have been led out of provincialism and narrowness and gained many of our concepts of honour, beauty, and heroism."

His library has the smell of old leather and smoke. Some days when I came to read to him, the room would be in a cloud of smoke. Whenever I think of Grandfather I can close my eyes, and I can smell a cigar as if it was right under my nose. I loved Grandfather and do not find the remembrance of the scent disagreeable.

Though Mother said that she appreciated Grandfather's cabinet de curiosités, she found the odour of cigar smoke so offensive that she visited his sanctuary but seldom.

One day when I came for my daily visit his crippled foot

was propped on his gout stool, his teacup was balanced on his waistcoat, and his eyes were closed, as if he had nodded off. His gold knobbed walking stick had fallen from its accustomed place to the floor. His pocket watch was not in his pocket, but was hung on his watch keep, as if he knew his time was up. It is there to this day, but though Papa wound it, it would never run again.

William interrupted my reveries with a request for me to help him open the metamorphic chair into the ladder so that he could retrieve a book with a particularly interesting cover. I remembered the day years ago when I had asked Grandfather to read me that very book. "Ah, Little Cygnet," he replied, "though the fore-edge painting on that book is very pretty you will find it uninteresting and not worthy of the time we will spend on it." And so I told William, "You can't judge a book by its cover." Then I regretted it, thinking to myself that I was beginning to sound like Nanny!

William insisted upon taking the book down. Although inside the cover there was nothing to keep William's interest, he pretended to be interested. I refused to read it to him because he is so hard-headed. Mother calls him "Tête Carrée," but her voice is not hard. "Hard Head" sounds softer in French, I guess.

I miss Grandfather very, very much. If I could have him back, I would gladly read to him all day long.

Dear Diary,

This morning the sunshine beaming through the casement window reflected diamond patterns on the white of the schoolroom wall. William was fidgety and resistant to education again today, so Mr. Austin-Brown released us early. As this may be the warmest day until next summer, I had a plan for my ride on Bess. I asked Clive to ride with me and he agreed that, indeed, Thunder needed exercise. My plan was to persuade Clive to leave the property and take an ages-old path to the site of an ancient settlement atop the hill only twenty minutes from our entrance gates—at a trot, that is.

Grandfather had once taken me there on one of his digging expeditions. He found a circle of stones that day, and he told me he felt sure that it was the foundation of a shelter for an ancient people who lived there even before the Celts. As they had no written language, little is known about them. I did not understand Grandfather's enthusiasm when he discovered the rusty remnants of a spear, until he exclaimed, "An encounter with an object which has had a previous life with an ancient person generates tantalizing conjectures." I would be as excited as Grandfather if I made such a discovery today.

Bess was trotting along, admirably keeping up with Thunder, but, of course, though Thunder danced restlessly, Clive was keeping him reined in. As we rounded a bend, before us in the road a vulture was feeding on the carcass of a rabbit. The startled vulture flew up directly in front of us. Thunder reared, but Clive kept his seat. Then Thunder's thoroughbred temperament overcame him, and he flew down the path at full gallop. Bess, being a gentle little mare by nature, didn't rear or even shy. Clive and Thunder were soon out of sight. Dashed were the pleasant fancies of exploration and adventure that had danced in my mind. Sorely disappointed I turned Bess back to the stable.

Clive, his face flushed, was already unsaddling Thunder by the time Bess and I reached the stable. The usually taciturn Clive enthused over Thunder's speed, saying he was certain he could win at Ascot if he ran as fast as he ran today. My suspicion is that Clive enjoyed allowing Thunder to race at such a rapid pace!

Disappointed, I returned to the Hall and offered to take William for a walk to enjoy the sunshine. It was so very warm that we took refuge in the shade of the grape arbour. The grapes looked ripe, a deep purple brushed with white. As I climbed to the very top of the arbour to pick a bunch of sun-ripened grapes, I remembered how as a young child I had played I was a monkey. I'd seen a monkey's picture in one of Grandfather's books and heard Papa's friend, who had gone to Africa, talk about them. I always liked the geography lessons about Africa. Engrossed in my reverie I failed to notice that

William was climbing after me. Great clouds suddenly engulfed us, and William lost his footing and fell to the ground. I heard his terrified cries and, looking down, saw a ghostly apparition looming over him. Concern paralyzed me—not only the ghost, but William's screams of fear.

Then I heard a concerned voice saying, "William, are you hurt?"

When the smoke cleared I saw that it was the beekeeper, swathed in clothing from head to foot and carrying his smoking apparatus. He also had a big sack in which he had captured a new swarm and was on his way to place it in an empty hive in the orchard. William finally stopped crying, though he had a little cut on his lip.

The beekeeper offered to put a little royal jelly on William's cut to aid its healing. William resisted this suggestion until he explained that the worker bees feed the queen with it, and that as a healing aid it's good for all sorts of ailments.

To console William, he offered a bit of honeycomb to chew. William has learned to love honeycomb because Mother gives him some when his nose is stuffy. Back in the nursery, William started crying anew the minute he saw Nanny. Nanny was extremely vexed that I had let William climb the arbour. He is her pet because he'll have father's title one day. I think that she's going to make a milksop of him.

At nursery tea tonight, when William bit into his Rambly Pambly pudding, it spilled on his shirt. I waited for Nanny to

The bee keeper capturing a swarm of bees

reprimand him, but she didn't say a word. Nanny complained that the battered crab at our midday meal was fatal to her digestion and she was feeling liverish. I guess that's why she is so crabby. I wish she'd take one of the blue pills she takes when she has a disordered liver.

Dear Diary,

William and I spent all morning in the schoolroom. William was not pleased, for he seems to have contempt for book learning, but I didn't mind even though I was reciting dreadful French verbs.

Evidently Mr. Austin-Brown still has not remembered the poem he promised to write about me. He did bring me some coloured chalks and suggested I draw a picture on the slate board of a flowering plant he had brought in from the garden while he worked with William. I was thankful Mr. Austin-Brown had the task rather than me. I think William bores Mr. Austin-Brown. I think he wishes he could spend all his time writing poetry. Nanny sniffs and says, "Beggars can't be choosers."

To please William, I decided to draw a bug on the stem of the plant. Besides, it made the sketch more interesting. But I had just finished my drawing when William grabbed the chalk from my hand and called me a dunce, saying that anyone knows all bugs have six legs and only spiders have eight legs.

He erased my eight-legged bug so vehemently that a nearby leaf was deleted. I was most displeased but said nothing because of the presence of Mr. Austin-Brown, thinking that surely he would reprimand him. William then drew a bug on my drawing of the plant. I thought he was going to spoil my drawing but he did very well. It looked exactly like the beetle he gave me for my birthday. Instead of a censure, Mr. Austin-Brown complimented him, saying that he could grow up to be an artist. But I knew, of course, that being the oldest son he will inherit the estate, so he'll have to spend his time supervising everything. I think he'd rather be a bug expert. Maybe he can hire a bailiff to look after the estate and then have time for his beetles. Unlike most landowners Papa does not have a bailiff. He likes looking after the affairs of the estate himself. Papa says that no leisure activity can compete with the satisfaction of the pursuit of a worthwhile task.

Mr. Austin-Brown asked me if I had received a letter from Papa and Mother. At the remembrance of my disappointment, I felt tears welling in my eyes. Mr. Austin-Brown reached across the table and put his hand on my arm. "But, of course, there has not been sufficient time to receive a letter. I know you were very disappointed not to be able to go to London with them."

With that I could have broken down in tears, but I didn't want him to think I was a crybaby. I simply nodded and swallowed hard several times. He took his handkerchief from his pocket and handed it to me. I blew my nose and said, "I hope I'm not coming down with a cold." Just thinking he understood without my saying anything made me feel warm, as if I were enveloped in a cozy blanket.

Dear Diary,

I think Nanny likes to take us to services, though not because she enjoys the sermon, for even with her ear trumpet she can't hear Cousin Hubert's oration, no matter how sonorous. I think it's because she enjoys donning her fanciest lace collar and best bonnet and sit in the family pew.

She wore the hat with the gauze veil today. In the winter she wears her feathered beaver bonnet over her lace cap. I'll be glad when Mother allows me to wear a bonnet. She insists that only a hat with a brim is suitable for one my age.

Nanny had Clive harness the pony cart to take us to the church. I think this is because William loves to hold the reins and pretend he's driving. I didn't like it at all when he flicked Bess with a whip because she was lacking a trot. After services William wanted to take a tour by the lakes and around the park. I insisted on walking back to the Hall because I think three people are too heavy for Bess to pull such a long way.

William is such a fidgety person. If he sits still through the service, he is rewarded by getting to play with his Sunday toy, the Noah's Ark. He is not allowed to play with it other days so that it remains special to him.

Cousin Hubert talked about Heaven today. Ever since Sister went to Heaven I've been wondering what it must be like. I think the angels will not be scary even if they have wings. Cousin Hubert says that the future world will not be controlled by angels but by our Saviour, who is a perfect leader because His temptations and suffering make Him able to understand and help us if we will only not let our hearts become set against Him. One thing I hope is that there will be a heavenly library where I will find all the answers. Grandfather once said that happiness is having interesting thoughts, but I think that in Heaven we'll really be happy because we will know the answers, not just the questions.

Dear Diary,

It's morning but I can't wait to tell you. Last night, because it was such a warm evening, I opened even the shutters to my window. I fell asleep while reading, failing to snuff my candle. I was deep in slumber when I was awakened by the brush of wings on my face. At first I thought it was just a dream, but then it happened again. At that moment, the candle guttered and darkness enveloped me. Wide awake by this time, I stared into the darkness. Then I heard the noise of something banging on the door of my bookcase.

I assured myself that it wasn't the ghost, for the ghost has never come into the children's wing, it being so new.

Then I just knew it was an angel. Maybe I have a guardian angel. By this time the moon had come out from behind a cloud and was shining through the window, but I could see nothing. And then it happened again—the feeling of wings brushing my face. I knew I should be braver, but I struck out. I was frightened when I hit something, so I started to pull the sheet over my head. At that moment I saw a shadow across the window.

It took me a long time to fall asleep, for I was wondering if I had injured my guardian angel.

This morning when I awakened, there I saw, sitting on my windowsill, a beautiful bird. I didn't know what kind it was, but it was beautiful and white. It didn't fly away, even when it saw me looking at it. From the pocket of my apron that I had hung on a chair, I retrieved a biscuit, intending to crumble it on the sill, but when I approached, the bird flew away. I watched to see where it would go, and it fluttered feebly to the ground. And there was Tobias, crouched low and creeping through the grass. Clive says he's a good mouser, but he catches more than mice. I feared that he had seen my bird, and that he would catch it and kill it.

Alarmed, I hurriedly threw my shawl over my nightdress and rushed outside. Tobias had disappeared, but my beautiful bird was still sitting in the path. When I approached, it fluttered, as if it was trying to fly but could not. I wanted to see if I could help it but when I held out my hand, it fluttered away

Tobias

deep within the hedge where I could not reach it. I wish it had trusted me, for I only wanted to help the beautiful creature.

Abandoning hope of helping my bird, I rose to return to the house. I then spotted Tobias near the corner of the conservatory, stalking an unknown prey. To my astonishment, it was Mr. Austin-Brown, ducking and dodging about in the most unusual manner. I could not imagine the purpose of his actions. His left hand was held aloft and he would move back and forth in and out of my sight. At first I thought he was practicing some new steps for a dance, but the lunges seemed too severe for that activity. He looked as if he were contesting some invisible enemy. At this moment, Tobias pounced, wrapping both his paws around his leg. This well-plotted attack tripped Mr. Austin-Brown, and he tumbled head over heels to the ground. I could not help but burst out laughing at this ludicrous sight.

He was startled to see me, and I felt regret that I had laughed. He might have been hurt. He picked himself up, I think a little embarrassed that I had observed his fall. Breathless, he could scarcely speak but hastened to explain that he was practicing his fencing, and sheepishly added that he must have looked foolish without a foil or an opponent. I quipped that he did indeed have an opponent, Tobias. He laughed, his expressive mouth revealing strong, even teeth. I liked it that he appreciated my attempt at humour.

I would like to learn to fence, but I think it would be most difficult to fence in a skirt. I'm sure Mr. Austin-Brown is expert at this art. He looked most graceful—until his fall, that is. I wish I were a boy so that I could fence with Mr. Austin-Brown.

Nanny dressed me down severely for going out of doors improperly clad. I don't understand why she was so upset. My shawl is large and I felt clothed with sufficient propriety. I think it was the fact that I ran into Mr. Austin-Brown that so upset her.

I would like to have a guardian angel. I don't know whether to believe there is such a thing as a guardian angel or not. Perhaps angels do not have to have wings. Cousin Hubert told me that sometimes there are angels pretending to be people. I thought and thought and I could not think of a single person I know who could be an angel pretending to be a person, unless it was Dearest Sister.

Dear Diary,

I was awakened this morning by the cockerel's crowing, so piercing to my ears it almost hurt. It's such a beautiful sun-shiny day, an orange day! After lessons Nanny gave me per-mission to take William out for a walk—with my promise not to go near the lakes, since Papa has not yet taught William to swim. Until we learned to swim, Dearest Sister and I always heeded Nanny's warning of the danger of drowning.

I remembered watching Tom teach Clive to swim. He threw him off the pier into the deep water. Poor Clive sank to the bottom and came up sputtering. He went under again and came up choking, coughing and flailing his arms helplessly. I had such fear that he was drowning that I grabbed a nearby oar and proceeded to extend it to Clive to save his life. Tom took the oar from me and declared that "sink or swim" was the quickest way to learn to swim. Sure enough he stayed afloat, but he swallowed a lot of water. My heart went out to him.

One hot day several years ago Dearest Sister and I begged Papa to take us down to the lakes so we could dangle our feet in the cool water. He agreed and to our surprise said he had decided that for our safety he would teach us to swim even if we are females. As I was the oldest I was to be first. I must confess that I was dreading the experience. Papa picked me up in his arms and started to wade out into the water. I was so terrified that Papa was going to throw me in the water that I clung to his neck like a leech. I cried and protested that I really didn't want to learn how to swim.

Papa finally carried me back to shore and said he'd teach Dearest Sister. In her calm way she followed Papa's instructions, holding her nose and putting her head underwater. Soon she was floating, with help from Papa, of course. They seemed to be having a wonderful time.

When they came ashore Papa didn't scold me, but took my hand and looked in my eyes and said in a gentle voice, "I will teach you how to swim when you decide you're ready." When I looked into his eyes I knew I could have perfect trust that Papa would never let me come to harm. I was ashamed that I had been so afraid that I had not trusted Papa, and I assured him I was ready.

He carried me back out into the water, and holding me in his arms he slowly lowered me to the water. He held me without effort, and I felt as if I was as light as a baby. His strong arms reassured me, and he coaxed me to put my head back and unclench my hands.

When I finally relaxed, Papa released me with only a fingertip on my back. I loved the feeling of the water supporting me. Before long I was floating without the support of Papa's hands. He then taught me to hold my breath and put my face in the water and float on my stomach. Finally, Papa told me to paddle like a dog. Goliath, who had heard our voices and come down to the lake, was standing on the pier, watching Papa and me. At this moment he dove into the water and swam out to us, splashing water in my face. This frightened me, and I found myself sinking under the water. Papa immediately supported me and laughingly said, "See, Cygnet, Goliath wants to show you how it is done." My confidence restored, I found I could stay afloat and dog-paddle myself.

Dearest Sister and I loved the days that summer when it was sufficiently warm to go swimming. Best of all was spending time with Papa, who accompanied us until we mastered the water. That was before Dearest Sister became too ill to go into the cold water. Papa said one must never swim alone, and besides, the activity lost its enjoyment without someone to share it.

Nanny warned William not to wear the red soldier's jacket Mrs. Taylor made for him, for it might make the bullock chase us. As William so loves playing at being a soldier, he refused to remove it and declared he didn't want to go beyond the ha-ha anyway. There went my plan to entertain him in the field, making daisy chains and puffing away the thistledown from the dandelions.

I decided to take him to the maze, as he loves to get lost in its avenues. I, too, used to think it intriguing when I was little. Of course, I know it by heart and no longer get lost. I don't understand why Mother and Papa's guests enjoy the maze. I would think adults could figure it out very quickly. I've watched them out the window; the young ladies, sometimes even not so young, act confounded, and seem deliberately to go down the dead-end passages and stop so that the gentlemen can catch them. I suspect that a tryst is the purpose of the activity.

We stopped to watch Thomas, who was trimming the bush that Papa had instructed to be shaped like a beetle in honour of William's birthday. Thomas kept grumbling to himself that it wasn't proper—that he's never seen a topiary shaped like a bug. But Thomas always has a scowl in his voice.

On our way back to the house we stopped by the cutting garden to pick flowers to take to Nanny. Some of the roses were in full bloom and ready to shatter but I gathered them anyway. William wanted to go to the herb garden and get some sorrel leaves to chew, but I was afraid he'd eat some of Mother's medicinal plants against which she has warned me.

I hurried William on to the orangery, where he loves to pretend he's in the jungle. I picked two oranges, one for Nanny and one for William and me to share. The espaliered nectarine tree had beautiful fruit, and William wanted one, but I judged them too immature to pick. He could not be dissuaded, and I must confess that I experienced a sense of satisfaction when he spit it out, complaining that it was too sour.

Once back in the children's wing I spread out the flowers to dry. I plan to mix the petals with the peels from the oranges and other herbs and spices. I think that mixing all these lovely fragrances will be most pleasing. I plan to place them in a dish in Mother's chambers to welcome her home. Mother will be pleased with my use of French when I tell her I have made potpourri to place in her cachepot. Tonight when I took my bath I put flower petals in the water. I loved the smell the hot water released. I must learn from Mother what she puts in her bath to make all the bubbles.

I think I will put a pot of honey by the fire. When it is hot I will put rose petals in it and allow it to cool. I hope that Mother will like honey that tastes and smells like a rose. One time our honey was so peppery hot that it irritated the throat when swallowed. Papa said the bees had been feeding on the flowers of nettles. He would eat it, but the rest of the family refused to.

Once, when I came out all over with rash from eating too many raspberries, Mother had me soak in a tub of water to which she had Nanny add carbonate of soda. I loved the slippery feel of the water, and besides, my rash went away.

Father likes salt in his bath. I tried it once, but it made my skin smart. Men must be different. Papa says only witch hazel or bay rum are suitable scents for a man. Whenever I think of Papa it seems I can smell those fragrances. I wish I would have a letter from Papa.

Dear Diary,

Mr. Austin-Brown left today for Cambridge to apply for admission to King's College. He was required to write letters in Latin to each of the electors signifying his intention of offering himself, to be delivered in person along with testimonies of good conduct from his prior school. Nanny says it's an exercise in futility, as he does not have funds sufficient to sustain him. I don't think Papa would approve of his leaving William and me for this foolish ambition.

Clive and Liz are planning to join a group from the village going to Worcester to attend the 125th Festival of the Choirs of Gloucester, Hereford, and Worcester. As it is under the patronage of Her Royal Highness and the Prince Consort, I asked Nanny if we could go to see our Queen. I thought this would appeal to her more than listening to the choirs, as Nanny is tone-deaf and does not enjoy music. She said, "Indeed not! There will be at least fifteen hundred people in attendance, and that's too large a crowd to fit into the cathedral. One could probably never hear a note of music. And just because the event is under the patronage of our monarch does not mean she will be in attendance. In fact, the papers have reported that the Royal family has already left for Balmoral."

Nanny insisted I work on my French verbs, reminding me that every lady has need of French. Mother is proud of her Norman ancestry, and informed me more than once that after the Norman conquest French was the language of our nobles and royal court for over six hundred years and that's why I must learn it. I much prefer history and even more I like novels. Novels are exciting because they are about people. I am reading one of Mother's books by Currer Bell, even though Mother says I'm too young to read worldly books. I have been interested in reading it ever since I read in Papa's paper that it is really written by Miss Charlotte Brontë, a minister's daughter from Haworth. She had to pretend to be a man in order to obtain a publisher. I don't understand what difference the sex of the author makes to the worth of the work.

Tonight for supper we had pease porridge, William's favourite. Nanny has taught him the rhyme:

> Pease porridge hot
> Pease porridge cold
> Pease porridge in the pot
> Nine days old.

William says he likes it all those ways. I think what he really likes is the game of clapping hands with Nanny when he says it. I prefer a mess of broth with a boiled fowl myself. Nanny likes a soup of vegetables with marrow or a clear turtle soup.

Papa says he'll take a joint of meat any day over soup. He likes to have something to sink his teeth in. I think he is so bursting with vitality he has need for substantial fare.

Though Mother eats daintily of whatever she partakes, her favourite is an egg from a young swan, boiled hard. When shelled the appearance is so beautiful, the white of such purity, it is almost as translucent as Mother's skin. She likes it with a nest of spinach and, as with all her vegetables, but little cooked. Mrs. Potts sniffs and says health is of more importance than fashion, and vegetables insufficiently boiled are known to be exceedingly unwholesome and indigestible. On the other hand, she says too rapid boiling can injure a soup. I cannot want to consume the egg of a swan, for the thought that the poor bird has been deprived of her egg. Nanny pointed out that I do not feel the same about hens' eggs. But swans are so beautiful and their eggs are so few.

Nanny reprimanded William for slurping his soup and gobbling his hot buttered toast. It made me feel triumphant to have him chastised for once. But then she found fault with me for handling my spoon with my left hand. If it is proper to use the fork with the left hand, I do not understand why it is not proper to do so with the spoon, especially when I am so much more agile with my left hand.

Life seems to be full of contradictions.

William was rewarded with his nightly lollypop. I fear that I find myself full of resentment. Nanny can be quite waspish.

Dear Diary,

After our midday meal I was roaming the house. William was on his dapple-grey rocking horse, Dobbin. Nanny was clapping her hands and singing "Ride a Cock Horse" to encourage him. I think five years is much too old to still be riding a rocking horse, even if it's a big one. He seems addicted to riding that toy. I think it's because Nanny used to rock him constantly when he was a baby.

In spite of the din, I heard the gallop of a horse and a knock at the door. Crawford brought a packet of letters from Papa, and one was just to me, and it was personal, for it was closed with sealing wax impressed with the family coat of arms.

Crawford's letter was lengthy, with instructions for the upcoming hunt season. I think I am getting old enough to ride to hounds, but I'll never be allowed to do so as long as I only ride Bess. As much as I love old Bess, I think I am old enough to have a more spirited horse. William can then ride Bess, because he'll soon be big enough for a real horse, not just Dobbin.

I went to the stables to exercise Bess and I passed the house of Mr. Horne. Since he is the huntsman, he has the largest and nicest house on the estate. He does not have any children, so he does not need such a big house. I wish he did have children. His hounds are not enjoyable to pet, because they are in a pen and they bark and jump around so much I wouldn't like for them to be out. I asked Mr. Horne why he was adding apple cider vinegar to the dogs' drinking water. He says it increases the dogs' endurance, enabling them to hunt all day without tiring. I told him Papa had sent a letter, and he said Father had written him, too.

The gamekeeper walked up and proudly dropped the lifeless body of an otter at Mr. Horne's feet. I could not but express my distress. Papa and I had on many occasions enjoyed watching the little otters as they playfully slid down a slippery bank of the lake. I developed a great affection for them, and Papa and I even gave them nicknames, Spanky and Slinky. I protested to the gamekeeper, "I understand the need to trap the weasels, stoats, and badgers, but why the otters?"

"We'd have no fowl to shoot if we don't save them from all

Spanky and Slinky

these vermin," he declared. "In your grandfather's day there were bustards to shoot, but now there are none. I've suggested to your father that, like some masters, we set traps for the worst vermin of all, the poachers. He says he won't be responsible for crippling some man, that there are laws that should be deterrent enough. Well, I know one gamekeeper who was shot by a poacher. Laws are not enough for some men!" With this he stomped off, his gaitered bandy legs stamping exclamation points.

Mr. Horne didn't have time to talk because he was so busy getting ready for the upcoming hunt season. Besides, he's a taciturn man. Tom, the groom, was out exercising the horses.

I had brought a carrot from the vegetable garden to feed to Bess. She's a sweet thing, and I felt regret I had wanted a faster horse. I found Clive in the harness house polishing the harness brasses. Clive didn't seem to have time to talk either because he had to ready all the harnesses and saddles and do all sorts of chores. Oh, well, he knows much about horses but he never seems to be given much to converse. Perhaps he is self-conscious because of his lisp. I guess he has no time to read books, though I know he likes music.

Last May, when a fiddler came around, I saw him dancing in the barn with Daisy, Liz's cousin. They were laughing and appeared to be experiencing great enjoyment. I wished I could have been dancing, too. Not only were Daisy's feet dancing, but her eyes as well. She would twist and turn with a flounce of her dress. Though boisterous in appearance, she is fair of face and keeps a straw in her mouth with which to pick her beautiful even white teeth. Nanny says it is not a ladylike thing to do. Daisy is so corpulent that her dress seems to be bursting at the seams; being a milkmaid, she eats lots of butter as well as her curds and whey. The best I can say is that she has lack of a genteel figure.

Clive's eyes were sparkling, and his cheeks were flushed from the dancing. He is a very bonnie lad. I am surprised that he likes to lark with Daisy even if she was chosen Queen of May. I think she looks as if she's sadly lacking in sensibility.

It is so exciting when Papa and Mother have weekend guests for the hunt. All the bedrooms are filled, at least all except our ghost's. The servants are all astir bustling about from morning until night looking exceedingly harried. Crawford reprimands them, saying they confuse activity with efficiency. The villagers Crawford has engaged are too busy, or perhaps it is that they are too meek to talk to me.

Even though I am not yet allowed to ride to hounds, just hearing the horses snort and the sound of the horn is exciting. I always watch from my window until they disappear over the brow of the hill, and the sound of the horses' hooves and the baying of the pack at full cry no longer resonates back to the Hall. I wish I could be riding with them. Even if it is more difficult for the ladies on their sidesaddles than for the men, I feel confident I can keep my seat as well as some of those I see.

Mrs. Potts will be busy for weeks, boiling plum puddings in bags and making mincemeat pies from the venison as well as other sweetmeats. Special dishes such as ox cheek dumplings, roast ducklings, a rack of venison, roast pig, and stewed eels will be waiting on the curved hunt table when the riders return. A Stilton or Cheshire cheese will be in the cheese cradle. Many will have had drinks from their stirrup cups, and they are usually in the best of humour.

The floors will have been polished with beeswax, and that evening there will be music for dancing or at least the hire of a harp. There will be fresh tapers in the candelabra on the table, and their lights will be multiplied in bowls of water. After dining the ladies will retire to the withdrawing room for a nothingness of conversation while the gentlemen remain at table with their cigars and port. They never tire of comparing the rival merits of the different breeds of hounds or of recounting the activities of the day, the ride or the shoot as the case may be. Though they admire the speed or wiles by which the fox has baffled the hounds, no one seems to care a fig for the fox, even when the hounds tear him to pieces. Surely it's not just the trophy of his brush or mask or paws. I guess it's the pleasure of the gallop and the exhibition of the skill of the horseman in taking a stream or hedge. Or could it be just that the pursuit takes their minds off their loneliness?

Before the fox hunting season there is grouse shooting, then the partridge season, and then the pheasant season, and after the hunt there is duck shooting. The unhappy part of these sports is that Mother and Papa are so often absent at the homes of friends for their hunts. I think I'd like best the "lawn meets," when people from all over gather, along with the hunters. Then there are breakfasts and dinners and even picnics, although I guess only men go on those. But, best of all, Mother says there are real balls with real orchestras with a piano, violin, and cello, and sometimes even a cornet. And they play not only galops and polkas, but waltzes as well.

I will be happy when I can ride to hounds and go on house parties, but I don't think I'll ever enjoy shooting a gun. They produce much too loud a noise! And I know I'll never enjoy spending a whole evening talking about each hedge or shot. I cannot understand why they would sit around the table when they could be dancing.

The days are full of tedium, and the hours have passed slowly since Mr. Austin-Brown has been absent in Cambridge.

I was so happy finally to have a letter from Papa. I wish I were in London.

My Dearest Little Cygnet,

The roads were exceedingly rough and difficult for our passage. Mother is extremely fatigued from the journey and pleased to take up residence in our town house to recover from the rigours of the journey. Travel does not agree with her delicate constitution.

I wish the railroad came closer to Primrose Hall. Perhaps that transportation could be less taxing on her strength. I hear the stock in the railroad company is in such demand that there will be quite sufficient monies available to expand the line—so perhaps one day soon we can easily come into the city even for a visit of brief duration.

As we entered the city we drove past the Smithfield Cattle Market. The mordant odors, even with handkerchiefs to our noses, were so disagreeable that Mother felt quite faint. It is no wonder the neighbours are petitioning for relief.

London is very crowded. So many people have moved into the city to work in the factories that there is no place for them to live. Whole families live in one or two rooms in dark, dreary cellars. Open sewers line most of the streets. Most of these workers are illiterate and don't attend church or chapel. They have need for moral and mental improvement, and to realize the value of hard work and self-reliance. They frequently fail to show up for work on Mondays because intemperance seems to be their only diversion. I fear many do not appreciate the importance of an education and do not allot the few pence charged for the schools recently established by the government.

The city has built wash houses, for which there is great need. The people have to stand in line for bathing and for washing their clothes. The streets are crowded with horses and littered grossly. Little ragamuffin boys wait to earn a pence or two by sweeping the way so that one's shoes will not become soiled. The dust raised by the horses' hooves from the cobblestones and the litter fills the air, and the odours are too pungent for health.

I have missed you here in London. I know you wanted to come but I am sure you can see that it is no place these days for a pretty one like you. There is much sickness. Both the typhoid and cholera are prevalent again and there has been an outbreak of smallpox. One sees funeral processions everywhere. I am happy that you are safe and healthy in our wonderful air in the country.

Your Mother sends you her love and says to mind Nanny and help take care of William. Here are kisses for yourself.

Your ever loving
Papa

Dear Diary,

To do as Papa asked, I offered to take William downstairs to play. As we walked down the staircase William, as always, wanted to stop and make faces in the convex bullet mirror, which distorts his image. To persuade him to stop, I told him he might freeze that ugly. We stopped on the landing to look at Grandfather's long case clock. William likes it because the decoration above the face has an officer atop a white horse, brandishing his sword with each swing of the pendulum. Grandfather had it made to celebrate the victory at the Battle of Waterloo. Grandfather told me his cabinetmaker made the case, but the works were made by a skilled Swiss family of watchmakers who fled to England to escape persecution because of their religious beliefs. Before that the family had lived in France, but they found it necessary to leave France when their trade collapsed because of a crushing tax the French government put on their clocks.

It seems religions and governments are more important than people.

Papa says the Romans used sundials and obelisks whose shadow on brass markers indicated the time. We have an obelisk in our garden that Grandfather brought from Rome. Papa explained that the Romans had brought it from Egypt back in the days of Julius Caesar. It's hard for me to realize that our obelisk is even older than when Jesus was born. It can't indicate the time because we have no markers in our garden.

I'm glad we don't rely on an obelisk to tell time. Not only are there too many shady days, but I like the friendly ticktock of our clock. It seems like the heartbeat of our house—almost as if it were alive. If only it could talk!

I fetched a twig basket from the pantry so that William could gather eggs, an activity he finds a source of amusement. Nanny cautioned us to watch out for snakes in the hens' nests. Clive recently discovered one coiled around a post, attempting to crush the egg it had swallowed.

Cook told us to keep an alert eye because the gypsies have been indulging in clandestine visitations to our poultry yard. They probably thought a sly varmint would get the blame, but Liz had seen their shelters in a shady nook, and, in fact, a gypsy fortune-teller had approached her cousin Daisy on the footpath to the village. Cousin Daisy had parted with a hard-earned coin to have her fortune told, and the gypsy woman had upset her by predicting that her affairs of the heart would suffer a serious and possibly permanent mishap.

Cook lectured to Liz that the danger of toying with the future is that the mind will deceive itself and make a reality out of a false prediction, and such activity may occasion a dire consequence or at best an unfulfilled expectation. Regardless of this comment by Mrs. Potts, I hoped that I would come across the teller of the future so I could query her about my future, and resolved to put a coin in the pocket of my apron on my next excursion.

Cook ceased her lecture when she noticed that William had lifted the cloth covering the kneading tub and was poking his finger into the rising dough. I thought for certain she would scold him, but she just laughed and said she guessed it was time to knead the remaining flour and liquid into the leaven for its second rising. Papa bought Cook an iron oven that came from America, but Cook says that even if it is the latest thing, for her bread she prefers the stable heat of her brick oven properly pre-heated with faggot wood. She added that she knows the precise quantity of fuel it requires and how long to let the oven rest before placing the loaves in it.

William and I stopped by the garden and picked squash bugs to feed the chickens. The usually dour Thomas approved because it helps save his squashes. A little red ladybird landed on my arm. William loved the tiny black-dotted beetle and wanted me to capture her so he could add her to his collection. I told him to let the little beetle live because ladybirds are beneficial to plants. To calm his loud protestations I told him that Cook says that a ladybird betokens a visitor. This did not suffice to quiet him so I chanted the little rhyme:

> "Ladybird, ladybird, fly away home
> Your house is on fire and your children will burn."

The little bug flew away. William wanted to know how I knew her house was on fire, and was I sure it was a Ladybird

and not a Lordbird. And why do we call it a bird, when anyone can see it is a beetle. William is such a literal person.

On the way back to the kitchen Maggie, having finished
scrubbing the clothes on the washboard, was hanging the
wash on the line. I walked to the herb garden with her, as I
wanted some lemon balm for my bath. She wanted to pull up
a few soapwort plants to make soap from the roots. The plants
were covered with delicate pink flowers, so I asked for the
flowers for the potpourri I'm making for Mother. Maggie says
the best soap for laundry is that she makes from fat and ashes.
It may get the linens clean, but it smells excessively strong. I
suggested she put lavender in it, but she pointed out the lavender leaves would make a mess of her laundry. I've been thinking that if the fat was heated and the flowers were put in it for
a period of time, then strained out before she made the soap,
the fat might absorb the fragrance.

As we went into the barnyard a big goose ran at us, angrily
flapping her wings and honking. William was terrified. I
removed my apron and, waving it, shooed her away. "Just wait,
you bad bird," I warned him. "You'll be a pretty sight at the
Christmas feast!" William, his courage mustered, taunted him
proudly, "Yes, you bad bird, you'll just end up a feather comforter for my bed!" The goose lost one of her feathers, and I
picked it up to save for Papa. He always acts like he's pleased
to get them, but I know he prefers the pens with steel nibs
because the ink flows better. Grandfather preferred the quill,

having always used quills. I think I will sharpen the quill and add ink highlights to my sketches.

William gathered all the eggs from the nests where the hens left the nest but was afraid to get the ones where the hen was sitting on the nest. I stuck my hand under the hens and got several more eggs. One hen had several eggs but she would not give them up, refusing to leave the nest, and squawked at us. I decided we were better off allowing her to hatch her eggs, and left them under her. The basket was completely full anyway. William begged to carry the basket. I gave it to him with the admonition to take care, but he paid scant heed. On the way back to the kitchen he was running and caught his toe on the root of an old tree and fell. Basket, eggs, and all flew in every direction, breaking almost every egg.

When we returned to the kitchen and Mrs. Potts saw what had happened, she said, "Well, there goes my cake. Let that be a lesson to you, Missy. 'Don't put all your eggs in one basket.' And you, young man—'Haste makes waste!'"

When I reported our misadventure to Nanny she advised, "Oh, well. No need to cry over spilled milk." Those two have a saying for every circumstance. I didn't want to be literal, like William, so I didn't comment that it was eggs we had lost, not milk.

Our supper tonight was not bountiful. Mrs. Potts had taken her roast from the fire and placed it on the kitchen table while she fetched something from the larder, but when she returned the joint had vanished. Cook was so shaken she didn't prepare a substitute. She is completely unnerved to think that any stranger would dare enter her domain. She is convinced one of the gypsies has stolen the meat. It seems strange that Cook has more fear of a real person than of a ghost.

Liz is frightened, and she is placing the blame on our ghost. Nanny is unusually concerned about the occurrence. I can tell because her voice is very high, as it gets when she's excited. She does not want to concern William, so she tries to act as if it is nothing.

It was the most pleasant of surprises that I had another letter from Papa today. If Papa were here everyone would feel reassured.

My Dearest Little Cygnet,

I met with the gentlemen from India with whom I hope to engage in commerce, importing hemp for making ropes. Your mother is still much fatigued, and while she is recovering from the journey I dined in the Reform Club in Pall Mall. The architect of the club, Sir Charles Barry, undoubtedly received the inspiration for his design from the Palazzo Fornese, which I visited several times in Rome back in my Grand Tour days. But as Nanny would say, "Imitation is the sincerest form of flattery!" He has also designed for several of our friends gardens in the formalism of the Italian tradition. The club is a magnificent building, but your grandfather would be most distressed because it cost £88,000, over twice the original estimate that he and the other members had budgeted. However, he'd approve of the library, because, though simple in decoration, it is massive, with room for the most extensive collection of books and periodicals.

It's a far cry from the days when the club was founded in 1836 for the exchange of the ideas generated by the Reform Bill of 1832, for which your grandfather worked so diligently that he was labeled radical by some. You can take pride in the fact that your grandfather not only was instrumental in passing the law to abolish slavery but, at the same time, initiated the fight in Parliament to repeal the Corn Laws. I wish he had lived long enough to see the passage of that bill. Those large tariffs on all imported grain benefited the landowners and agricultural workers, but were a severe hardship to all other labourers.

He was never afraid to be in the minority when he felt he was doing what was right. Under discussion in Parliament this week was the slave trade in which some ships sailing under our Union Jack are engaging. There is no doubt that your grandfather would speak up against such activity.

Chef Alexis Soyer, whom your grandfather was instrumental in bringing from France and who is famous for his culinary flamboyance, was regrettably absent. He is, however, to be commended. Not only has he run soup kitchens for the poor here in London, but he has now gone to Ireland to help feed the starving. Tell Mrs. Potts I am bringing home his latest cookbook as well as a jar of one of his sauces, for which he has developed a brisk market. I wish she could be here to see his all-gas kitchen, which not only is a task-saving device but enables him to control the temperatures, insuring an excellent product. I like the man even if he is a Frenchman. He has great initiative, for which I have as much admiration as I have for his culinary prowess. But most of all, I admire him for his concern for the plight of a people who are not even his own people.

After dining I was entertaining myself with a game of Patience when three other members asked me to accommodate them by making a fourth at a game of Whist. I would have preferred to play Loo, Commerce, Speculation, or even Pope Joan, as round games tend to be more convivial. But after only *two rubbers I found I had won quite a pile of fish. It's easy to see how one can become addicted to gaming, because it's most enjoyable when you win. My pleasure was greatly diminished, though, when one of my opponents could not accept his loss with equanimity and good temper. In a quest of a war of words, he, being landed, expressed surprise and disdain that I would con-sider engaging myself in trade. I replied that I would be pro-viding employment and needed goods, expanding the economy of our country, and in the end benefiting his life as well as my own.*

Help Nanny with William. With her lumbago she cannot get around as she once did. Your Mother sends her love and says she already misses you and William.

Your loving
Papa

Dear Diary,

With the damp, Nanny's lumbago is still hurting her, so to do as Papa asked, I decided to entertain William. He's too clumsy for hopscotch and skipping rope. There was not enough wind to fly his kite. He wanted me to ride with him on the seesaw, but I'm too old to be sitting on a seesaw, and so I pushed it up and down with my arms. He soon tired of that, as did I.

William was amenable to my suggestion that we feed the parrot, so we went by the kitchen to get a biscuit. Mrs. Potts was trussing a partridge, and the forcemeat kept falling out. William asked her to make the orange jelly she used to make for Dearest Sister when she was ill. She said it was not possible—that she no longer had any of the good Russian isinglass. She has refused to procure the Italian form of isinglass, saying it appears to be some form of purified gelatin, but certainly inferior, with no restorative power for an invalid. She did promise that she would make his jelly the very next time a calf was butchered, as she could prepare the jelly from the calf's feet. She was more than a trifle out of humour, because she was in acute discomfort with a toothache. She unlocked the spice box to get a clove to chew to alleviate her pain. I love all the wonderful smells emanating from the box. While she was getting the biscuit for William I put a few cloves and a cinnamon stick in my apron pocket to add to my surprise for Mother.

Biscuit in hand, William and I went to the conservatory where Polly has lived for more than thirty years, ever since Papa's Uncle John brought him from Jamaica to Grandfather. Great-uncle John didn't have the opportunity to enjoy Polly, as he was killed in the Battle of Waterloo. Poor bird! He must miss his bird friends back in Jamaica. If I were a bird I'd want to be free to fly high, high in the air. He greeted us with his usual "Hello, don't bite!" When I was five years old like William, I was feeding him a biscuit and he bit my finger so hard that it bled. Ever since then I've tried to teach him to say "Don't bite the hand that feeds you," but the obstinate thing will only say "Hello, don't bite." He never tires of saying "Polly wants a cracker." I don't even know what a cracker is. It must be some foreign food. I had William be very careful when he offered him the biscuit so that he would not suffer the same fate as I had.

I resented the poor creature for biting me until the day Ainslie followed me into the conservatory and, being his usual pesky self, started barking at Polly. Polly screeched and squawked, but Ainslie continued jumping up and barking at him. Suddenly, Polly flew down from his perch and pecked the persistent pest on the nose. Tail between his legs, Ainslie fled the conservatory howling in pain. I felt Ainslie had earned his just reward. Ever since then I have had a warm feeling for Polly. Besides, his feathers are beautiful, and the colours so brilliant, and he is entertaining for strangers. It's just that I wish he could carry on a conversation instead of repeating the same silly phrases over and over.

I returned William to Nanny and went down to the stable to see Clive. He wasn't there, but I waited awhile and finally he came running from the direction of the dairy, his hair looking like a hayrick that had been in a windstorm. I wanted to talk to him, but he was in a fret, hustling about doing his chores, as he was going into the village this evening.

The mystery of the vanished joint is solved! On the way back to the house I saw Goliath in the herb garden digging in one of the herb beds. As I neared, he growled at me in his deep guttural voice. I laughed when I saw that he was retrieving a large joint of mutton. I ran to tell Cook and quipped to her that Goliath must have thought his dinner too bland and needed improvement with the addition of spices. Mrs. Potts didn't appreciate my witticism as much as she does her own.

Goliath has been banned from her kitchen.

Nanny made me work on memorizing the catechism. Cousin Hubert is coming tomorrow to test me, as the Bishop of Hereford will be coming soon for the laying on of hands. Nanny does not require William to do memory work.

Dear Diary,

The day was fresh but fair.

At church this morning the sun was shining through the stained-glass window, which shows Jesus walking on the Sea of Galilee. It was placed there in honour of Grandfather's brother Godfrey, who was killed in the Battle of Trafalgar. Papa told me his body was draped in a flag and delivered to the sea.

The rays of the sun made a coloured picture on my white gown. The words of our hymn today were based on Psalm 146. It drew pictures in my mind. I was thinking that God gives us good things: peace, beauty, order, design, balance, and colour—a beautiful world.

Cousin Hubert's sermon was also based on Psalm 146. When he said we could praise God with prayer I remembered Dearest Sister, who always remembered her prayers both morning and evening.

When Cousin Hubert said we could express our praise through recitation of a Psalm, I thought of Nanny. She is a big believer in memory work. Then Cousin Hubert said we could praise God with writing and poetry and I thought of Mr. Austin-Brown. I don't remember his poetry ever mentioning God, but it is music with its cadence and beauty of words. I am certain God must like it. When he reads it I find the timbre of his voice most appealing. God must too.

When Cousin Hubert made the point that we could express ourselves through singing, I thought of Mother. Surely her soprano is so beautiful it honours God, whatever the words. I fear I croak like a frog in comparison. When I complained of my lack of beauty of voice to Papa, he laughed and hugged me and said, "God loves all creatures, including frogs, Little Cygnet."

I am thinking Papa praises God the best way of all. He is so vibrant and exhibits exuberant energy and does so much good for others. Besides, his merriment makes happiness wherever he goes. He enjoys the world so much God must be pleased. I cannot think of anything I do to praise God, since I really do nothing well.

> Please, dear diary, forgive
> the ugly inkblots on this page. I failed
> to pay sufficient attention and I knocked over
> the inkstand and spilled the inkpot. Mother would
> be most unhappy if she knew that I marred the
> beautiful journal that she gave me.

I thought about asking God to help me be less clumsy, but decided I should not ask God to do something I should be able to do myself. I think it's really up to me. Nanny is always cautioning me to look, to watch what I am doing.

Dear Diary,

Cousin Hubert, normally possessed with such reserve, was in high spirits as he left today to visit the place of his birth. Well, at least high spirits for an ecclesiastic. I hope that his distress will not be too severe when he sees his home, as Mother told me that his brother, who inherited the estate, found it necessary to place all the furnishings of the house at auction at Christie's to raise the money to enable him to retain the land. Cousin Hubert's competency is a sum insufficient to enable him to take a wife, in fact, hardly enough to keep body and soul together. Though it is desirable to have a dowry, his bride will not need a large allowance now that Papa has given him a benefice. Papa said Cousin Hubert could never make a farmer so it was not prudent to give him a glebe. Mother was pleased because she says Cousin Hubert not only would never make a farmer, but as he has no head for figures, would not succeed at commerce.

Cousin Hubert is Mother's second cousin once removed. He is the youngest son of six children, so his oldest brother, of course, inherited what is left of his family's estate. One brother is in the diplomatic service in India, another brother purchased a life appointment as an officer in the Royal Navy, and one brother went to Barbados to manage a coffee plantation. His mother and younger sister live with his oldest brother in the family home. Mother said that Cousin Hubert is as poor as a church mouse because his father was a wastrel. Papa replied to her, "It is a pity Hubert's grandfather did not entail the property so that it could not be encumbered with a mortgage. The income from the property would have been a more than sufficient livelihood. Your cousin may not have been a destitute rogue, but it was unforgivable that he was so lacking in family pride that he reduced his family to penury." But then he added, "Blood is thicker than water, and even if Hubert is once removed, he's still family."

Now that Papa has awarded him a benefice, he will have a living for life. Papa says it's good Cousin Hubert didn't have the money to go to Oxford, for he'd probably have ended up a Tractarian. Those vestments and all that ritual smacks of popery to Papa. He also is glad he did not attend Cambridge, because then he might be a Dissenter. Though they do good works, all that talk about conversion is not for Papa. Papa says that, as for him, he was born a Christian and will die a Christian and that the Church should be open to anyone who accepts basic Christian beliefs.

Cousin Hubert plans to visit in the homes of some of his cousins to seek a wife to bring him felicity. I think he would like to marry his cousin Alice, the daughter of his mother's sister. His Aunt Marie is married to a man who made a fortune with his gin distillery. Cousin Hubert will be attending many dinners and possibly even balls. It is a pity he could not have attended our recent dancing instruction, as his excessive height prevents him from being a naturally graceful dancer.

Cousin Hubert seems quite old to me, but Mother says that thirty-two is not really that old to be marrying. I had expressed to Mother that I hoped his bride will be young so that we can be good friends. Mother said that the age of his bride is less important than that she be of good character, ready to please her husband in all matters: to laugh at his little whims, to never weary him with accounts of household difficulties, to never be careless in attire or the arrangement of her hair. She should be careful never to forfeit his respect and remember always that the husband is the head of the household. At that, Papa tweaked a tress from under her lace cap and responded, "She must realize it is in the wife's hands to make the home a place of peace and happiness." They both laughed and looked at each other as they do.

William and I will now have to postpone our religious and moral instruction until Cousin Hubert returns, hopefully engaged to such a lady.

In my prayers tonight I made a vow if one day I should have a husband that I would make our home a place of peace and happiness. And, if it was His will, to please make Cousin Hubert's wife young enough that I can have her as a friend.

Dear Diary,

This morning I was beckoned from sleep by the song of the catfinch that was perched on a bough outside my window. I went to my window and he continued to sing as if he were glad to see me. The sun shot rays of gold through the leaves of the tree. The sweet smell of new-mown hay filled my nostrils. In the distance I could see the horses pulling the mower flicking their tails to keep away the flies, and the haymakers piling the hay into the hayricks in their white work smocks. It was such a warm day I was sure they were enjoying their beer, and I knew Nanny would not permit me to go to watch them.

Last year, when I went to the fields, the farmers were cutting the ripe corn with their sharp sickles. They were tying the sheaves together to make shocks to be piled into a cart and taken to the barn to be winnowed. At midday the farmers retired under a tree to drink their beer and eat bread and cheese with their wives, who had brought their midday meals.

A poor old woman and a little girl in the most ragged of clothing came to the field to glean a few grains that had fallen to the ground. The feeble old woman was sadly tired with stooping, so I impetuously took one of the sheaves and gave it to her. Her worn, wrinkled face broke into a smile as she kissed my hand. But when Nanny learned what I had done, she was exceedingly displeased with me and said I must not associate with such people as gleaners. She said the old woman should go to the poorhouse, and she forbade me to ever go to the fields again without her permission.

It was too beautiful a day to stay inside. I walked towards the lakes, which were shining with the glimmer of the sun on the water. I could hear the lowing of the cattle standing in the lake, looking at their reflections in the shallow water. Fluffy cloud sheep drifting in the sky looked down at the sheep in the meadow. I checked the weir between the lakes to see if there were any fish so I could tell Mrs. Potts. There was one large pike.

I was fascinated watching the path of a dragonfly as he hovered over the water, gracefully exploring one plant after another. The reflection of the sun on his iridescent, translucent wings made him beautiful. I wonder why he is called a dragonfly when he looks nothing like a dragon, and he wouldn't hurt a fly.

A good word for my vocabulary copybook today is <u>misnomer</u>. To call a dragonfly a dragonfly is a <u>misnomer</u>. But then that would be cheating, as I already know that word.

I walked over to the boathouse. If Papa had been here I would have begged him to take me out on the lake. While I have no particular passion for fishing, I love to go out in the boat and watch Papa, because his enthusiasm when he catches a fish is a pleasure to me. But it seems a long time now since the last time he took me out.

I remember that Papa caught a beautiful trout. The fish's sides glistened silvery, washed with soft orange, and his shiny black back looked as if it had been sprinkled with gold dust. I thought that he was too beautiful to die, but Papa took a knife from his pocket, sharpened it on a stone, and slit open the fish's belly. There inside were two perfectly intact little fishes staring wide-eyed, expectant, as if they had not realized what had happened to them. When I expressed my horror Papa said, "Cygnet, it was their destiny. You must be realistic. Those little fishes are possibly this beautiful fish's own babies." With that he grabbed my arm and said, "And I think I'll eat you!" and pretended that he was going to take a bite out of my arm. I squealed in protest, but in truth I like it that Papa loves nonsense so cordially.

That very same day we saw the pair of swans who fly in to spend every summer on our lake. Papa told me that swans live a long time, and they mate for life like people do—or should. We heard one of the swans singing an exceedingly beautiful but mournful song. Papa explained that a swan sings his most beautiful song as he is dying. My heart was very sad for the poor swan who will be left all alone without her mate.

I looked today in the weeds along the shore for the nest of the swans. It was well hidden and I never spotted it, but I watched the mother swan, so graceful with her long slender sinuous neck, swimming in the lake. Three little cygnets were swimming behind her looking so very drab and ungraceful.

And then I wondered, unhappily, whether that is why Papa calls me Cygnet.

I walked the long way back to enjoy the air. As I passed through the wilderness, I felt as if eyes were watching me. When I looked into the undergrowth I fancied I saw a large form lurking in the shadows. But when I looked the second time, I decided that it was simply an effect of light, for it was gone. But I hastened my steps. As I neared the church I heard a sound, which I took to be that of a newborn lamb. Once close I saw that there on the steps of the church was a basket containing a bundle wrapped in a faded flannel cloth thin from washing. I pulled back the cloth and was shocked to see the red face and naked body of the tiniest infant girl. Her eyes were shut, and her little mouth was working as if she wished to suckle. One of her feet was badly deformed. My heart was lost to the unfortunate babe who had been abandoned.

Picking up the basket, I hurried home to the kitchen. Mrs. Potts was as shocked as I was and immediately sent Liz to summon Nanny. There was much speculation as to who had left the baby. With a quaking voice Liz declared that the ghost must have left the baby, as it could not be anyone from the village because she would know any woman expecting a child. Mrs. Potts was sure it must be one of the gypsy women who did not want the babe, as she was deformed. Nanny thought it was some stranger passing through the countryside. I blurted out that we could keep the baby. We had plenty of room and I would help care for her. Nanny declared emphatically that that was an addlebrained idea, and she sent Liz to summon Crawford. When he arrived there was further discussion about the identity of the mother. They all agreed that whoever the mother, she was indeed sinful and wicked.

Crawford immediately took matters into his hands, and made the decision that the infant should be taken to a hospital for foundlings in the city. Cook insisted that the baby could not make the journey without nourishment, and she soaked a clean cloth in watered milk with a bit of sugar for the tiny one to suck.

I was completely dissolved in tears as Crawford left for the stable with the basket in his hand.

Nanny chided me that I was being very sentimental and totally impractical. Under her breath she muttered, "One is enough," and she chided, "Let me hear not another word about this from you!"

Mrs. Potts saw how upset I was, and she declared that it was highly unlikely that such a tiny baby would survive and that, if I were to become attached to the infant, it would only be more painful to lose her.

With that I cried harder than ever. I was so upset that for once I was poor in appetite.

I was going to pray for another letter from Papa, but it did not seem proper to make so selfish a request when the dear little helpless babe needed my prayer. I prayed to God to look after the wee one, who faces a dismal future, as she might never find husband or employment because of her deformity, and could end up like the pitiful old woman gleaning in the field.

Perhaps God thinks it would be best if she did not survive this life. She may not have been born a Christian like we are, but surely God would not hold that against her. Cousin Hubert says we are not born Christian, but how can she have an opportunity to become a Christian if she does not survive?

I wish Papa were here. I do not think that he would send the infant to the hospital for foundlings.

Dear Diary,

I finished reading the novel I borrowed from Mother's book cabinet yesterday. Fearing that I have been laggard about doing the lessons that Mr. Austin-Brown assigned to be completed by the time of his return, so I spent the morning in earnest endeavour. I would not want to disappoint Mr. Austin-Brown yet I feel that he expects too much. William has no assignments, which is not fair.

Nanny asked me to entertain William. Her lumbago is hurting her, as it is raining today. He wanted to play the music box in the withdrawing room, mostly because it has the sound of a snare drum and while it is playing he marches around with a swagger stick pretending he is a soldier on parade. Mother's father ordered this special instrument from Switzerland and had his cabinetmaker build the box. Inlaid on the top, in several colours of wood, is a medallion of musical instruments. The magical instrument plays ten different tunes. My favourite is the "Rip Van Winkle Waltz," but William likes the marches. As the tune was played, I was engaged with watching the strikers, so beautifully enameled with flowers and bees, when William, without permission, started winding the crank vigorously. Before I could stop him, the music stopped. I fear he wound it too tightly, for it would no longer play. Mother will be most upset when she returns, and I feel responsible.

I then took him to the gallery and let him roll his hoop the length of the gallery. The clumsy child let the hoop escape and it ran into a <u>torchère</u>, which instead of a candle held a porcelain vase with Grecian figures around it. The vase fell to the marble floor with a loud crash and was broken into pieces. I know it is a cherished possession as Mr. Wedgwood gave it to Grandfather. I fear William does not realize that some things are so special they are worth caring for. I can't decide. Was it William's fault for letting his hoop get away, or could it be mine for letting him roll the hoop in the gallery? Nanny definitely thinks it is the latter.

Late in the evening Tom came to the kitchen and reported that there is no government-supported hospital for foundlings in Hereford, nor even in London. The government discontinued their support a great many years prior, with the reasoning that the indiscriminate acceptance of foundlings with no effort to discover the identity of the mothers was promoting immoral conduct. At this point Nanny and Cook nodded their heads and clicked their tongues. Tom went on to tell us that he had located an Asylum for Waifs and Strays, and though exceedingly crowded with young children of all ages as well as babies, the good people had accepted this poor unfortunate baby. They are members of a religious group, not from our Church but from Scotland.

I bowed my head and silently thanked God for the good people who care for the children no one wants.

With the tedium of the absence of both Cousin Hubert and Mr. Austin-Brown, the days seem endless. Mr. Austin-Brown has been gone much longer than I thought he would be. I know no secret can be hid from God, and since God can hear my very thoughts He knows I wish Mr. Austin-Brown would return. I have never before been so eager for lessons.

Even if I didn't pray yesterday for a letter from Papa, one arrived today. It is so full of news I feel as if I've been to London myself. I will say "Thank you, God" in my prayers tonight.

London, September 10, 1848

My Dear Little Cygnet,

Now that your mother shows signs of recovering from her fatigue, she and I have found time to enjoy the pleasures of the city. Yesterday we visited Kew Gardens. I was amazed how much has been accomplished since Her Majesty gave the gardens to the people. The orangery is filled with the most unusual and rare plants from all around the world. We visited the Museums and the newly constructed Palm House. Under construction for several years, it is an amazing accomplishment. The director, Sir William Hooker, has written a pamphlet with impressive information about this structure. It is 362 feet long, 100 feet wide, and 60 feet in height. There is even a spiral stair to mount to a gallery in order to view these magnificent Great Plants at their summit. To temper the too-powerful rays of the sun, the glass is tinged with green at the suggestion of our acquaintance, Mr. Hunt of the Geological Survey.

Palm Court Kew

The Tower

But most interesting of all is the heating system. Under the flooring there are 24,000 feet of 4½-inch pipes and 1,000 feet of tanks filled with hot water provided by a stove heated with underground furnaces. The smoke from these furnaces, twelve in number, will be conducted 479 feet from the stove through a brick tunnel six feet high to an ornamental stack or tower with a large reservoir at the top to supply the water. It is 96 feet high and at such a distance that it does not distract from such a magnificent structure as the Palm House.

I enclose my quick sketches of the marvel so that you can show them to William and explain it to him.

As we left Kew we stopped by a roadside vendor of blue and white English delftware—golly-ware, as Grandfather called it. It is old-fashioned, but Mother had eyed a posset pot in which to minister her medicinal mixtures. I found it easy to be persuaded, for if your mother covets an object, its value is beyond practicality. Indeed, she already possesses more than one posset pot. However, I spied a most practical purchase. You know how cold your mother's hands get in the winter attending services in our frigid church. This vendor offered handwarmers fashioned in the shape of a Bible, with an opening in the ceramic spine into which hot liquid can be poured. Now she can always attend services assured of comfort.

We made a call upon our old friends, the Harts. As well as visiting with them, I wished to inquire if they knew of a position available for Egbert, who wishes to live in London. As his parents live here I can understand his desire. In fact, I admire him for his devotion. Since he was very satisfactory as a footman, I will give him a sterling reference.

When we arrived I found Mr. Hart absorbed in studying his play on his chessboard. When I apologized for interrupting his game, he replied that he was in no hurry, as his opponent lives in Amsterdam and they are conducting their match by correspondence.

The Harts report that their son, J.B., has written from America that gold has been discovered in California. Though a promising journalist, he now plans to sail to Panama, take a wagon across that country to the Pacific Ocean, and there find passage on another ship to California. Though this route will shorten his journey by thousands of miles, it is but a muddy mule trail through a rain forest lousy with disease, wild animals, and deadly insects. They hope he will change his mind. His impractical desire of last year was to go to Texas because it had become a State in the Union. Mrs. Hart was so apprehensive that his real purpose was to join General Taylor's volunteers to fight in the United States's war with Mexico. She was greatly relieved when the Guadalupe-Hidalgo Treaty was signed.

Mr. Hart confided to me that his wife's over-mothering is what drove his son to seek adventure. Mr. Hart said that he would like to think that since he had travelled so much farther down the road of life and knew its pitfalls that his advice would be worthy of his son's respect. I advised him that there comes a time when one must let go of one's son and realize he must make his own decisions, however foolhardy they may seem. I only hope this latest adventure will not be a "wild-goose chase." If I were young I might think I would relish the adventure, but as a happily married family man I find sufficient of interest here in England.

I thought of you when we visited Vauxhall Gardens last evening. There were thousands of lamps—well, at least hundreds. Though not the fashionable place it was in our youth, there is still plenty to entertain one. The bands and singers would have set your little feet to dancing. William would have loved the jugglers and the comical one-man band. He had bells on his hat, cymbals tied on his knees, a harmonica in his mouth, and a drum tied to his waist.

The only mishap of the evening was that Mother lost her favourite purse, the stocking purse of silk net decorated with steel beads. I was not certain but that she had been the victim of a pickpocket. She was most distressed, but I assured her we'd procure a new one. Mother has decided Vauxhall has indeed become too crowded and vulgar.

We are saving a visit to the Menagerie of the Zoological Society at Regent Park for a time when you and William are with us. They recently received from India a Bengal tiger, a cobra, and a mangouste, or "egg breaker." They are said to be so rapid that a mangouste has been known to kill a dozen full-grown rats in less than 1½ minutes. With one of those creatures our barn would have no need for the rat catcher with his ferrets. Tobias will need to sharpen up or he could lose his job.

About twenty years ago your grandfather and I visited Regent Park to see a giraffe, a gift to King George from Muhammad Ali Pashal, the Ottoman viceroy of Egypt. The beautiful huge eyes of the unique creature sadly looked down at us from the sling that had been rigged to support her, as her crippled weak legs could no longer do so. She died a short time thereafter, in spite of the twenty-four gallons of milk provided her daily. Her attendant had placed an amulet containing verses from the Koran around her neck to protect her from the evil eye. Grandfather declared that Muhammad Ali Pasha was the evil one himself. He captured every year from deep in central Africa thousands upon thousands, probably as many as fifty thousand, poor souls and sold them into slavery or put them into his personal French-trained army.

Since your mother enjoys the theatre, I plan to send Egbert around today to procure tickets. Between St. James's, Drury Lane, the Lyceum, Sadler's Wells, and Surrey, surely he will meet with success. We are hoping to attend a performance of <u>Othello</u> or <u>Midsummer Night's Dream</u> instead of an importation of some farce from France. Since it is not the season, I'm not sure all the theatres will be open.

Unfortunately, Miss Jenny Lind, the Swedish singer who was appearing at the Haymarket Theatre, has left the city to perform in Scotland; and so we will have to hope to hear her beautiful voice on another occasion. Tell Cook that Mother is procuring for her the receipt for the potage constantly prepared for Miss Lind by her own cook. It may not be responsible for her beautiful voice, but is reputed to be most delicious. Tell her it will probably not be as good as the superior soups which she makes. I will bring the pearl sago back with me when I return, as I know she will have the egg yolks, cream, and beef stock it requires.

Later

Egbert came back with tickets for The School for Scandal, which is playing at the Haymarket now. We're invited to the opera at Covent Garden tonight. In the city it is easy to procure amusement.

I am hoping to go to a house sale at the Duke of Buckingham's residence at Stowe. The contents have been under the Christie's gavel daily for over a month now. As the original part of the home was built during the reign of Queen Elizabeth, there are many objects of value and greatest variety occasioning spirited bidding. I read in the Illustrated London News that a portrait of Nell Gwynne fetched one hundred guineas. If I had been there, I would have much preferred to purchase the two five-legged armchairs made of solid ivory. To my mind they combine rarity, history, and beauty and, best of all, fetched but forty-three guineas.

They are said to have once been the property of Tippo Saib and to have been presented to Queen Charlotte by Warren Hastings, the first Governor General of India, during the time that his trial was impending. Mr. Hastings, who was charged with high crimes and misdemeanors, was found not guilty on all charges. Though his name was cleared, he was ruined in fortune, his wealth swallowed by the expenses of the seven-year trial. Against his private character there could be said not one word of reproach. He was simply a political scapegoat for the crimes, real or imagined, of the East India Company. He died venerated by English, native, and Anglo-Indians alike, for it was his genius and wisdom during his distinguished career of forty years in India that held our Empire together. Though impoverished, he must have greeted death a happy man, knowing that he had used his life well.

In great haste but with deepest affection,
Papa

Dear Diary,

A grey day; the weather is quite inclement! Since I was confined to the house I decided to engage Crawford in converse. His father was in service as house steward to Grandfather, and he lives in the same rooms his father occupied, the best apartment in the servants' wing. He almost never goes into the village or leaves the property. Sometimes I consider him an old frump, but Mother says he's dedicated and wants the house to operate efficiently. She says he's a gem and she couldn't do without him.

I found him in the butler's pantry, tenacious in his task of polishing silver with a raw potato dipped in carbonate of soda. Mother takes the plate with her when she goes to town for the social season, but as this was just a quick fortnight trip she left it so that it could be readied for the upcoming hunt season. His face, withered like an apple that has dried up, was pursed in concentration upon his task. His pinched nose, elevated in the air, always gives me the impression that he has detected an extremely distasteful odour. I wonder if Crawford simply enjoys polishing silver, or if he feels that others will perform the task insufficiently well.

I like it when I can persuade him to regale me with tales about the olden days, when our house was first built, over seventy-five years ago. It wasn't big then, as the south and north wings had not yet been built. What an exciting time that was to live. I don't think I would ever be bored.

He was dry in converse today and could not be persuaded.

But he did introduce me to Bridget, the new chambermaid. I've never known anyone to have hair like hers. It is exceedingly curly, more orange than a carrot and less red than a beetroot, and very wanton. Mother's Abigail could try all day and never be able to dress her hair in the latest styles. Her eyes are green with yellow flecks in them like Mother's peridots. The colour in her face is so high that her cheeks would never need to be pinched to be rosy. Her upturned nose is plentifully sown with light brown freckles. I did not think she was at all pretty until she smiled and then her face was radiant. Since she has not yet had time to make her uniform from the serge Crawford provided her for that purpose, she was still wearing her homespun wool dress that hung from her thin frame. She had rolled the sleeves up above the elbows to better perform her tasks.

The weather necessitated postponement of an excursion about the property.

Though experiencing great difficulty understanding her, as she does not speak the Queen's English with ease and has a heavy Irish accent, I learned she is one of eleven children in her family. She has never been away from her family before, but had to leave because of famine caused by the failure of the potato crop. Her brother went to Boston in America, and she wishes she could have gone with him. She seemed exceedingly morose. To comfort her I told her to be happy she is in England, because they still have slaves in America and England abolished slavery over ten years ago. This upset her, because she then worried that her brother would not be a free man. I had to assure her that Massachusetts didn't have slaves. It was only the southern states. Besides, all the slaves in America are Africans. I didn't know this for sure, of course. My effort to be helpful certainly backfired. Trying to think of something else to make her happy, I offered her one of my books. She said she'd like to have one if there were lots of pictures. Finally I came to the realization that she was not able to read well enough to enjoy a book. I found one of my old picture books to loan her.

I looked through the library to choose a new book to read. Nanny thinks it is not good to read too many books, especially poetry and fiction, because she says books form the bent of the mind. But Grandfather said books guard the truths of the heart and straighten the mind. Mr. Austin-Brown says books should not be read for amusement, but thoroughly. He wants me to read only the books he assigns. Sometimes I ask him questions he cannot answer, and he says he will look them up. He can read Latin and says that when William is older he will teach him Latin as well.

I wish Mr. Austin-Brown would return, because I always enjoy our discourse and he never speaks in Latin to me.

Tonight I read Mother's book by Mrs. Charlotte Smith, no matter what Nanny thinks. It has no pictures, but I don't mind, for I like having my own ideas of how the people and places look.

I thought about Bridget, and I was thankful that I had an interesting book to read and candles to read by. Some people have no candles, because they are very expensive, I'm told.

Dear Diary,

It was an overcast day with a strange metallic cast. I went upstairs to Mother's chambers to watch the workmen hang Mother's new rose-sprigged wallpaper, but they had completed the task and departed. The coronet over Mother's bed looked strangely naked without its draperies. I wonder if she plans to replace them, or if she has ordered a French bed to go with the fauteuils that she brought from Paris on her last trip.

I am always sorry when Abigail is absent in London with Mother. I like to talk to her because she reads books and, even better, she can dress hair in the latest fashion. When she has time, she curls my hair with the curling iron and makes me look very grown up. She puts some of Mother's hair jewellery in my hair for me to admire in Mother's silver-framed toilette glass on her dressing table. She even lets me use a little of Mother's rose lip salve.

I opened the drawer in Mother's dressing table to find the lip salve. Her jewellery case was there, and I found that she had taken most of her jewellery with her to London, but I put on the bough bracelet whose working of gold simulates wood. And I pinned on the brooch, which is formed in the Algerian knot and set with cabochon garnets discretely engraved. I wanted to wear them, but for fear that I might lose them I replaced them in the case.

When I tried to replace the case, the drawer would not

open. I pulled and yanked and the drawer finally opened but the whole table shook. Off went Mother's toilette glass to the floor with a crash. The looking glass was broken into pieces. I was horrified. Not only would I have seven years of bad luck, but Mother will be most displeased.

At first I thought, "I won't tell anyone and the paperhangers will be blamed." But I know Nanny would tell me that that would be a sin of omission, if not commission. The last time Nanny caught me in a prevarication I was assigned the task of writing the proverb "Lying lips are an abomination to the Lord" a hundred times. And it was but a little fib.

Though it was getting late I decided to get Mother's parasol and go walking in the rain. The sky was overcast but it was warm. The wind was still, as if God was holding his breath waiting for something to happen. It started to rain, and I loved the feel of the silken rain on my face. By the time I reached the pond the raindrops were splashing on the water, making little round patterns on the surface of the water. Then it came to my attention that the sky had darkened. At first I thought time had passed more rapidly than I had realized. Then I noticed very dark clouds had blown in from the south. I decided I must return to the house.

Suddenly, dark scudding clouds descended and the wind picked up. The wind was so strong that debris and rain were blowing across the path. I hurried. The rain and wind seemed to harshen, and even though I stooped, the rain blinded my eyes. I was finally to the nearest shelter, the gardener's shed, and just as I reached for the door, like a bolt of lightning, a silent white figure flew by my face, chilling me with a blood-curdling scream. I rushed to get inside. As I stepped inside another white figure flew at me with a hiss. Wings were arched over its back and it was flying right at me. The ghost? And not one but two? I tried to be brave but my skin was crawling.

Terrified as I was, I felt I must run to the house and escape. I bolted back into the rain. And suddenly right in my path there was the ghost, fluttering and hovering above the ground as if to prevent me from proceeding to the house. The wind and rain hindered my vision, and as I ran the wet arms of the ghost tackled me and I fell to the ground. A face with a malevolent aspect looked down on me with hooded dark eyes and a gaping empty mouth. Bumps like the skin of a goose rose on my arms and legs. I was frozen with fear. A gruff voice said, "That owl musta gave a fright to make yer run right into that sheet. Hie ye to the house and owt this rain or yer'll catch your death." Only then did I realize I was entangled in a sheet Maggie had left hanging on the line, which was being whipped by the wind, and that the toothless grin belonged to Thomas, the gardener. Still trembling, I disentangled myself and ran all the way back to the house. Nanny was very angry because my clothes were soaked and because I had made her worry and had taken without permission Mother's best parasol which, Nanny scolded, is meant to protect a lady's face from the sun, not the rain. Besides, I had completely ruined my shoes. I didn't have to confess to the broken looking glass; Nanny had already discovered the mishap and was most displeased. It was a relief to my tongue that a confession was unnecessary.

When Nanny came to bring me a cup of marjoram and lemon tea to ward off a cold, I told her about the owls. She responded, "That's what you get for reading those morose and ghoulish novels. Let that be a lesson to you. It's not a profitable use of your time to read such tales of terror." With that she took the book by Mrs. Charlotte Smith off my bedside table. I had seen one of Mrs. Ann Radcliffe's horror novels in her canterbury in her sitting room. Knowing that Nanny was not practicing what she preached, I resolved to keep books hidden beneath my pillow in the future.

As I write this, I hear mournful hurting groans and sounds like the cry of a baby. Sister and I used to think it was our ghost, but reason says it is the wind howling around the corner of the house and sawing and fretting through the oaks.

I am afraid to go to sleep, for I am fearful that my terrible nightmare will visit me again tonight. I dream that I am aboard a vessel with huge sails, whipping in a furious wind. Mountain-high waves break over the bow of the ship and all of the passengers are screaming in terror. I am very, very small. I see Papa and I cry and reach out for him. He tries to come to me but is always beyond my reach. A huge wave breaks over me and I cannot breathe. It is then that I always awaken.

When I would have my nightmare, Sister used to climb in my bed and hug me. How I miss her. Sometimes I pretend she is still alive, and I whisper to her that I am sorry for all the minutes I wasted. I imagine what she would think, and then what she would say. It keeps her alive and lessens my guilt for all the thoughtless hurts I must have inflicted.

It has not been a good day and I cannot think of anything felicitous to be thankful for today. I feel very peeved at Nanny. She is as stiff as starch. Even though she tells me she has my best interests at heart, she could be less brittle in temperament.

Dear Diary,

Now that the storm has passed, the air is clarified as if the whole world has been washed. When I looked out the window I saw that my old friend, the largest oak tree in the garden, had been blown over, its roots like arms with fingers entwined reaching for the sky.

I wondered if the squirrels were in their nest in the hole in the tree when it fell. I thought of how I would feel if my home blew away and I was left without the security of my comforter in my bed. And there on the ground destroyed by the fall lay the bird's nest, which I had watched the mother robin build with care. First she brought grass, twigs, and strips of bark. Next she deposited beakfuls of mud and debris, after which she squatted down and vibrated her body for a few seconds, moulding the mud into a deep cup. With each beakful she again performed her squat vibration, then turned her body a few degrees and repeated the behaviour. By the end she was making as many as sixteen turns within the nest. When the cup was completed she lined the molded cup with fine grass and even included strands of thread, which had fallen from Mother's basket as she worked on her embroidery in the garden. All this time the papa bird sat on a limb and softly sang. I wondered why the papa bird did not help her and how she knew how to build her nest. It was home to the little warblers all spring.

I remember the concern I felt when I watched the fledglings being urged from the nest for their first flight. The smallest bird fell to the ground with a thud. I was fearful Tobias would capture him before he could flutter to safety, and I thought the mother bird had been most cruel to her babies, but now I realized how necessary it was for them to become independent.

As I watched, a little hedgehog came out of his home in the storm-whipped yew hedge and was nosing around the upturned dirt, enjoying a buffet of insects. I decided against showing him to William and Nanny, because if I told William he would want to go out and gather bugs for his collection. If I showed him to Nanny, she would say, in her nasal voice, "It's an ill wind that blows no good." Besides, I am feeling quite peevish and cross with Nanny. She is entirely too crotchety.

I remembered with pleasure how I used to tie a coverlet between the limbs of the tree and lie shaded up in the boughs as the sky peeked through the leaves, happily reading a book in my bower. "Oh well," I told myself, "I'm too old to climb trees anymore." But then I thought of how Mr. Aesop's fox decided the grapes he couldn't reach would be sour anyway. Of course, it is a terrible loss. The garden will never look the same, at least not in my lifetime.

I went to the kitchen to ask Mrs. Potts if we could use the dishes with the Aesop's fables characters on them today. She was in ill humour because she was out of the good German yeast Mother procures in London, and she had found the yeast from the nearest brewery so extremely bitter that it could only be rendered fit for use by frequent washings, which would take several days. Bridget came into the kitchen about that time and volunteered to show her how to make dairy bread, which is frequently made in Ireland when it is impossible to procure yeast. She said that all she would need is buttermilk which has become quite acid and carbonate of soda.

Cook sniffed and said with a snort that she didn't need to be shown how to make any Irish bread. She was certainly capable of a perfectly good unfermented bread without risking the outcome on rancid buttermilk. She uses sesquicarbonate of soda and muriatic acid of the shops. Bridget protested that she had been warned that muriatic acid is poisonous.

Cook frowned and said that Bridget was showing her deplorable ignorance about cooking. Only fifty drops are added to a half-pint of water, and when it is mixed with the sesquicarbonate of soda the leavening is created, rendering the muriatic acid harmless. Of course, Cook added with pride, you have to know that no salt is needed, and understand how to handle it for the oven.

I saw Bridget's face fall. I know she was eager to be helpful. I don't know whether it was Cook's pride or her contempt for the Irish that made her so insensitive.

Cook readily agreed that we could have our nursery tea served on the Aesop's Fables dishes. She said they were just old crockery anyway, maybe as much as one hundred years old, since they belonged to Great-grandfather. William will be pleased, because he always likes for me to tell the fables which go along with the illustrations. I like the plates because they remind me of the fables Grandfather used to tell me. He once commented that any tale that has lasted almost two thousand years is bound to be of value.

To make Bridget feel better, I showed her several of the plates and told her the story of the fox and the crane.

The ancient stories made me think of Moses being found in the bulrushes and I thought again of the little foundling. What if Pharaoh's daughter had refused to take the baby Moses home to the palace? I wonder if God had a plan for our foundling at Primrose Hall.

Another newsy letter from Papa awaited me. How I wish he were here, so we could discuss the fate of the poor little baby.

Dearest Cygnet,

I did not take pen in hand yesterday, as Mother and I were so occupied. Your mother and I visited Edward of Holborn Street to place an order for a vanity case for her. The ability of their craftsmen is unsurpassed. Hers is beautifully carved and adorned with silver. We will be well equipped for our next journey, as your mother insisted that I had need of a <u>nécessaire de voyage</u> as well as her <u>nécessaire de toilette</u>. I had hoped to take your mother to Paris last spring, but it was reported that angry proletarians pursue the carriages of the rich through the streets, and mobs are tearing up the cobblestone streets and building barricades. No nephew ever owed more to his uncle than Louis-Napoléon. We have considered Rome, but as there is insurrection in Italy as well as Sicily, both such journeys seem imprudent.

I paid a visit to the boot shop on Bond Street to be measured, and the cobbler promised that new boots will be ready and waiting for me on my next visit.

I visited the Gunmaker Company, with only the intention of viewing the 1735 repeating air gun, made for King George II, which is on exhibit. I became interested in purchasing a Clarkson sporting repeating rifle but instead ordered a double-barrelled sporting gun made by William Moore, a fine craftsman. Tell William that I'm saving for him the fowling piece Great-grandfather had made in Edinburgh back in 1770.

We visited Madame Tussaud's Waxwork Museum of famous

people and found the personages amazingly lifelike. We proceeded to Trafalgar Square and the National Gallery of Art, as we wished to see the exhibit of the pictures of Mr. Joseph Turner. In front of the Museum, they have installed what the papers report is the first electric light in London. While the illumination produced is most excellent, I expect that the poisonous fumes of noxious gas produced from the batteries will forever preclude its use in dwelling houses. Holders of gas property, who seem to be in such panic about this, need have no fear of displacement by this costly experimental toy. I'm sure it is an impractical passing fancy. We had looked forward to seeing again the dazzling sunshine of the Turners, but they are being shown in the new Vernon Gallery, where it is so dark that one can scarcely see one's hand before one's face. I feel Mr. Vernon would never have given the money for this gallery had he realized how ill it was to be expended.

We next called upon Mr. Franz Xaver Winterhalter, famous for his paintings of many noble ladies on the continent. Because of the insurrections in Berlin and Austria he has come to England. It was our intent to commission him to paint a portrait of your mother, but to no avail. Since he painted the portrait of Her Royal Highness with the Prince of Wales last year his commissions by members of the nobility are so numerous that he has insufficient time and we must need look elsewhere.

I told Mother that if she treasured a true correctness of likeness we would visit Mr. Antoine Claudet, whose daguerreotypes are very coveted since he brought the art from France to London nine years ago. Mother said, "I've seen those. Please, I would rather my portrait be flattering."

While I feel she is always beautiful, she prefers her profile, and agreed to visit a Mr. Firth who executes amazingly detailed silhouettes. While I'm content with those cut out of black paper, Mother says she prefers a silhouette executed on glass or ivory.

On our return, a curiosity-monger approached me and attempted to sell me the sword carried by Lord Nelson at the Battle of Trafalgar. I told the man to be off, as any fool knows that Lord Nelson never used such a weapon at the Battle of Trafalgar. Your grandfather, who assembled an outstanding collection of curiosities, would trade only with men whose reputation and integrity were without question.

We visited the bookseller and, remembering how you used to enjoy Edward Lear's pictures in Grandfather's _Punch_ magazine, I purchased for you Mr. Lear's _Book of Nonsense_—the lithographs are as amusing as the verses—and, for William, Heinrich Hoffmann's _Struwwelpeter_. But tell William to fear not, for it has been translated from German into English. Both are just off the presses.

The bookseller showed me a most interesting just-published folio of lithographs of the Oregon Territory in North America. The sketches were done by Captain H. Ware, whom our government sent there three years ago because of the controversy with the United States over the sovereignty of that Territory. By the time he returned to England the dispute had been settled, but at least we have his pictorial record of this strange and wild but very beautiful country. Your grandfather would have procured it to go with his folio of the Plains Indians by Mr. Catlin.

Your mother purchased The Ladies Flower Garden by Jane Webb Laudon, which has beautiful hand-coloured lithographs. Mother was reading to me the essay on how to dress when cultivating roses, which may mean Mrs. Taylor will have to engage another seamstress.

I wished to subscribe to Mr. Charles Dickens's newest novel, Dombey and Son, but it was already over-subscribed. The bookseller told me the monthly installment is selling up to 40,000 copies. I contented myself with subscribing to Mr. Thackeray's Vanity Fair, which is selling at a rate of but 5,000 copies a month. My friends, however, advise me it is time more profitably spent than on Dombey.

For our library I indulged in purchasing Mr. John Gould's Birds of Britain, which, by the way, includes about seventy illustrations again by Mr. Edward Lear. His illustrations are remarkable, in a style at once spontaneous yet precise but, best of all, with a measure of his own whimsy. Remember the bird of prey I was unable to identify for you? Now, Cygnet, when you query, "What kind of bird is that?" if I don't know, we can look it up together.

I was distressed to see the increase in the cost of books. The new tax on paper makes books excessively expensive. Such an ill-considered tax! Reading should be encouraged rather than discouraged. Without language a people can degenerate into a primitive ignorance.

Mother is faring passing well. She sends her love.

Your ever loving
Papa

Dear Diary,

It is Sunday, but since Cousin Hubert is gone and William has the croup, Nanny said our morning prayers would suffice. I wanted to invite Bridget to join us, but Nanny said it would not be appropriate because she is Catholic. She added that she was sure Papa would not have offered her employment had he realized it.

Nanny had me read from the <u>Book of Devotions</u> Cousin Hubert had given me for my birthday. William was very bored and started making disturbing noises. Nanny of course couldn't hear him, but I felt he ruined the worshipful attitude we were supposed to exhibit, so I stopped and complained to Nanny about his behaviour.

She asked him to stop and he did, but then stuck out his tongue and made faces at me as I read. She pretended not to see him, but cut our devotions short. Nevertheless she permitted him to play with his Sunday toy, which I didn't think was just. She's only teaching him that his ill behaviour warrants no penalty.

The reference in the reading today was from Paul's letter to the Romans, where he says each person has gifts by Grace. I cannot think of a single gift I have. William has a gift—that of irritating me!

I encountered Bridget on a stroll after our midday meal. To escape from the wind, which had become quite challenging, we sat on a bench in the walled garden while we talked. I told her about the little foundling and how Crawford, Mrs. Potts, and Cook all thought that the mother was wicked and sinful to abandon her child. We both agreed that Liz was a nitwit to think a ghost had left the baby. Bridget offered that the unhappy mother may be a poor heartbroken girl, abandoned herself, who has no husband, no way to care for the baby, and only wants a better life for her than she could provide. Perhaps she hoped that Cousin Hubert, being a man of the cloth, would take the baby and raise her as his own. I wonder if Cousin Hubert would have kept the baby even if he had a wife.

The herbal borders, which Thomas plants as a discouragement to the insects, I found a comfort to the senses, for the pungent odour of the manure mixed with leaves in the compost was exceedingly unpleasant. Bridget said the smell was not offensive to her, as it reminds her of what her father used to say—"You can't take away without putting something back."

As we sat there, a little snake slithered from beneath a pile of bell glasses that had been stacked against the wall after they were no longer needed to protect the tender early spring plants from the cold. Bridget jumped up on the bench in alarm, as she had never seen a snake before. She explained that since the days of St. Patrick there had been no snakes in Ireland. I reassured her to have no fear, for it was only a little grass snake. I picked it up and tried to persuade Bridget to hold the harmless creature. When she refused I was sorely tempted to put it down her dress, but I thought that if I feared snakes I would not feel kindly toward someone who would play such a prank. I like Bridget and want her to be my friend, so I resisted the temptation.

I don't see why Bridget couldn't come to our services. Catholics have the same God as we do. Cousin Hubert said that Christ died on the cross for everyone—Tractarians, Dissenters, even Calvinists. Surely "everyone" means Catholics as well.

I don't care what Nanny says. I don't think Papa would send her away just because she is not a Protestant.

I prayed tonight for the unhappy mother who could not keep her baby, and asked forgiveness that I had never before given a thought about her. She needs prayers as much as the baby does.

Dear Diary,

I overslept this morning, not awakening until Bridget brought me my hot water for my morning ablutions. I was glad for the moment that Papa was in London, because he believes that early rising counteracts the tendency to sloth. Once I'd awakened I queried Bridget more about her life in Ireland. I learned that it is one thing not to have candles, and quite another to have insufficient food to eat. I like her frankness of manner.

Nanny complained she had heard the clock on the stair landing strike every hour, and sleep had totally escaped her. She declared that it was because the sheets had lost the smell of lavender. After breakfast she dispatched me to the fragrance garden to pick some fresh lavender to put in the linen press.

The air was clear, the kind of genial day when every breath is a pleasure. When I walked down the path under the arch of branches of the lime trees, I remembered how we persuaded William it was a magic tunnel. Once I reached the fragrance garden I thought of how Sister and I had played "Let's Pretend" in the garden. The pansies with their little faces were our audience, the rose arbour was the castle, and the buzzing bees were the Prince's subjects. One day William found a very big beetle, and Sister convinced him it was his "knight in armour." Our fingers were the actors: Sister would be a lady in a flower dress, and I, a snapdragon dragon, would attack and snap my jaws on the finger lady. Then the hero of our drama would leave his rose arbour castle, blow on his trumpet flower, and ride up on his steed—William's stick horse—and rescue Sister's flower lady. Because Sister and I had allowed him to caper about in his bare feet, for once he cooperated. When a butterfly would flitter overhead, Sister would say, "Oh, look! The fairy godmother has come to change the ragged dress into a dress fit for a Queen." We were never bored because we had each other. Though Sister was never strong, she always had the strength to use her imagination. I'll never stop missing her.

I sat on a bench, remembering how Grandfather used to enjoy sitting in the sun after his eyesight failed. As he once taught me, "Venus governs the rose, Jupiter owns the oak, basil and rocket belong to Mars." I'll always remember his wise words: "Learn to be attentive, for what you experience, no man can take away from you. Let everything which goes in your nose, your eyes, or your ears come out the end of your pen. You will find something extraordinary that needs to be expressed."

Tilting my head to the sky, I closed my eyes and let the rays of the sun strike my eyelids. I could smell the fragrance of the thyme planted between the stepping-stones, which my feet had crushed as I walked, all intermingled with that of the salvia, the tuberoses, the fragrant climbing roses on the treillages, and most of all the clovelike scents of the carnations. I could smell the mingled scents so acutely that colours passed through my closed eyelids. It was a wonderful scent I wish I could capture for bathing. I'd like to take a bath every day. I don't understand why William hates baths.

I had volunteered to pick some nasturtiums to bring to Mrs. Potts to chop into the butter on our cress tea sandwiches, and decided to share some of Nanny's lavender for addition to our tea biscuits.

Mrs. Potts told me to advise Nanny that when she can't sleep she drinks a tea made with lemon balm, so I gave Nanny some of the lemon balm I had gathered.

I'm going to ask Mrs. Taylor to give me a piece of lawn left from my dress, and I'm going to make lavender sachets for Nanny to keep in the drawer with her nightdress. I think I'll even decorate them with rosettes. I'm getting better at making the rosettes. I guess Nanny is right when she said, "If you don't succeed at first, try, try again."

I was very disappointed that I had no letter from Papa today.

I prayed that Nanny would like the sachets, and like me better.

Dear Diary,

When I awakened, I lay abed listening to the mournful cooing of the doves wafting from the dovecote. William wanted to go to the piggery to see the new piglets that have just been born. I dislike going there, for I find the odour extremely distasteful, but to please him we went. An enormous sow was in the pigsty nursing twelve little newborn piglets. I used that as an opportunity to drill William with his sums.

William climbed up on the fence to better observe the sow with her little piglets. Before I knew it he was making a game of hanging from the top rail, clinging with his chin. The solemn eyes of the sow glared at him with distrust. I impressed upon him that he must give up his dangerous mischief, and warned him the sow could kill him if he slipped and fell into the sty.

The little pink piglets are cuddly-looking and William wanted one for a pet. I had to point out that his pet would grow to be as big as the sow and wouldn't be so cuddly then. By this time he was so cross with me that he flew into a passion, and ran all the way back to the house. He latched the gate so that I could not catch him, as I had to walk around to the front of the house. A most exasperating child!

When I reached the house he was in the drawing room, frantically pulling on the bell rope with an impish grin on his chubby countenance. When he saw me he jumped into the lolling chair and curled up, putting his feet on the upholstery. This is one time I think that Mother would not fail to reprimand him, as she is most punctilious about our household. Nanny came running from the pantry in spite of her lumbago. Instead of scolding him, she invited him to come to the kitchen to play chemist. She mixed carbonate of soda with vinegar into water in a glass jar, and we watched it boil and fizz.

I suggested we could make an erupting volcano mountain by adding cherry juice to make the water red and burying the jar outside in a dirt mountain. Nanny didn't approve of my suggestion. "It would stain William's clothing," she declared emphatically. "You must learn to be practical and stop falling in love with a notion just because you are the one who thought of it."

I find William's want of conduct most vexing. Once, when Mother objected to Papa's discipline, he told her that if William was not bridled while a little chap he would get himself into trouble when he is older. Papa has need to remind Nanny of that.

This afternoon Nanny caught William playing with the lucifer matches. She took them away, but barely scolded him. Nanny thinks everything William does is amusing. I do not. I think he can be a little Lucifer himself. I decided not to give her the sachets I spent all morning making.

Dear Diary,

With Mr. Austin-Brown gone, I feel it is my responsibility to help William with his lessons. He is having trouble learning the alphabet, and he reverses his letters. I decided to play a game with him. I guide his hand and we write a letter of the alphabet. He thinks of a word that starts with that letter, and I finish the description in rhymes. The idea was that once we had worked our way through the alphabet I would transcribe it so we can read it together tomorrow. My hope was that because he created it he would have more interest in learning his letters. At first he thought it was great sport, but soon became impatient if I could not immediately make the rhyme. I was equally determined that it should have proper rhyme and cadence.

A is for Ants in a line on the ground
B is for Butterflies who go fluttering around
C is for Caterpillars, butterflies to become
D is for beetles rolling balls of Dung
E is for Eggs, insects lay them too
F is for Frogs who give warts to you
G is for Guns Papa loves to shoot
H is for Hogs who love to root
I is for Ice cream, a special treat
J is for Jelly we all love to eat
K is for Kippers which Papa adores

L is for Lions, it's said that they roar
M is for Moths who love candlelight
N is for Nanny who teaches us right
O is for Owls who hoot in the night
P is for Parrot, watch out or he'll bite
Q is for Queen, Victoria is ours
R is for Railroad, we'd like to ride for hours
S is for Spider, catching flies in her web
T is for Tigers, who eat people, 'tis said
U is for Umbrella to use when it's raining
V is for Voles we know from their digging
W is for William who likes wasps and worms
X is a letter we just have to learn
Y is for Yew Tree with dark glossy leaf
Z is for Zoological Gardens, with tigers to see

William, in a most petulant way, told me I was stupid—
that frogs didn't give one warts—it was toads. When we came
to I, he wanted ice cream, but I told him that Cook couldn't
make it, since it had been such a warm winter and hot summer there was no ice left in the icehouse. After that William
stubbornly lost interest and would not try. I lost my patience
and simply filled in the blanks by myself, which was of course
not the purpose of the exercise. But even worse, I didn't keep
my temper. I told him I would be glad when he went to Eton,
because he needs the rigours of discipline.

I went with my anger to Nanny, complaining that I was at outs with him and I'd never try to help him again. She commented, "Well, Missy, you can lead a horse to water but you can't make him drink. And I think you'll learn that an angry word may be sweet in the mouth but it will be bitter in the stomach."

I might have known I'd get nothing but words of wisdom from her.

Bridget told me she never had the opportunity for formal schooling. It has occurred to me that perhaps Bridget would like to master her letters. Instead of spending time with ungrateful William I will offer to teach Bridget.

Poor Bridget was in great distress. William, as usual, escaped censure.

Bridget is the first Catholic I've ever known. I must ask her about her beliefs. They must be very different if the guild refused to admit her father. I wonder if he could have been a member had he renounced his beliefs. Cousin Hubert says God knows the sincerity of the person. I think He would understand if a man only wanted to feed his family.

Tom is most upset that Clive never returned to the stable. He said that he knows Clive is stupid, but didn't believe that he was stupid enough to have thought that Thunder was the horse to be entered in the race. Lord Lyon's man left in a huff for Hereford, most displeased indeed.

I inked some of my sketches with the quill pin. I think I ruined some of these. I see why Papa prefers the steel nibs.

I thought Mr. Austin-Brown would have returned by now. It would be nice if he had written me a letter. For company, I read all my letters from Papa over again.

Dear Diary,

Nanny asked me to entertain William, as it was raining today. I decided that, with Mr. Austin-Brown gone to Cambridge, I had nothing better to do. Besides, Papa would be most pleased with me if I put my vexation aside. Papa told me that if you allow someone to make you angry, you have let him conquer you.

William wanted to play hopscotch and leapfrog, and I am much too grown up for those games. It made me very homesick for Dearest Sister. We loved card games and word games. We never tired of the dollhouse, which now looks so empty in the corner of my room.

To amuse William, I agreed to play hide-and-seek as long as he hid only in the smoking room, the morning room, the withdrawing room, or the dining room. I hid in places easy for him to find me. When it was his turn to hide, I looked for him in his favourite places: behind the leather screen, which he loves because it is tooled with gilded smiling fish, in the fireplace behind the dummy fire screen, under the draped table, and behind the window drapes. I looked in all the places I could think of, but William was nowhere to be found. I even proceeded to look in Grandfather's library in the hidden compartment painted to look like books on a shelf. William knows he is not to enter the library unaccompanied because of all the delicate and irreplaceable items. I decided William must have hidden in another of the rooms he knows is off limits. Or perhaps he had even gone out of doors just to frustrate me. I was completely irritated.

To teach him a lesson, I quitted the search and decided to return upstairs. I was halfway up the staircase when I heard a muffled cry from the direction of the dining room. I returned there and found the sound was emanating from the cellarette. I had not even thought to look there, for it is scarcely big enough for anyone to hide within, and besides it is customarily filled with wine bottles. The lid had jammed, and even with the most extreme exertion I could not open it. I heard loud banging noises coming from the scullery, so I ran there to get someone to help me. It was Liz, pounding the sugar to make powdered sugar, and she abandoned her task to help me. Try as we would we could not open the lid. Bridget heard our excited voices, and when she saw our predicament she ran to get one of the glazier tools. Only with her assistance were we finally able to pry up the lid. There was William, red faced, panting, and perspiring. I was startled. The imprudent child could have easily suffocated. Then I felt stupid that I had not checked the cellarette. I would never forgive myself if anything had happened to my brother.

After William awakened from his nap I amused him by making hand shadow pictures on the wall. He wanted me to read to him, and I let him pick the book. I don't mind reading stories to William if he lets me select them. But today I surrendered my desires to him. He chose <u>Tom Thumb</u> and <u>Dick Whittington's Cat</u>. Nanny likes me to read to him because then she is free to read or do what she wants to. At age five, <u>Cinderella</u> was always my favourite. I used to imagine I was Cinderella and a handsome prince would come and we would live happily ever after.

William may be a big pesty baby and lots of trouble, but he is family and my brother. I prayed that God would continually bring to my consciousness the sinful thoughts I have committed these past days so that I may feel remorse for not thinking of my brother with love.

Dear Diary,

Nanny sent me down to the kitchen to ask Mrs. Potts to prepare cress sandwiches for tea today. The aroma of gingerbread
baking filled the kitchen. Mrs. Potts had just finished trussing
a hare, and was hanging bunches of simples from the herb garden on the rack behind the chimney. Liz was tying some flowers and herbs tightly together with soft wool yarn. She
explained that two days ago her sixteen-year-old cousin Daisy
abandoned her employment at the dairy and ran away to
Gretna Green across the border in Scotland to marry Clive,
her sweetheart. This explains Clive's disappearance! It was a
shock to me, for I had no idea their attraction was any more
than a silly flirtation. Daisy's parents are muchly angered
because, even though it is no longer the law that persons
under twenty-one cannot marry without parental permission,
they have heard that in Gretna Green the blacksmith performs
the ceremonies instead of a cleric. Liz said that the village is
such a gossipy place that this was making quite a stir.

As they are due to return any day now, Liz was making a
tussie-mussie for her. It was centered with a red rose, which
she tells me stands for love, and which she encircled with
other herbs—the rosemary for fidelity, the marjoram for joy,
the sorrel for affection, the mint for cheerfulness, the verbena
for faithfulness, and the sage for esteem. She had stripped off
the lower leaves and tied the stems together tightly with the

soft yarn. Mrs. Taylor had given her a bit of riband, linen, and lace with which to frame the tussie-mussie.

Mrs. Potts joked, "Well, don't put any bachelor's buttons in the bouquet, Liz. That stands for celibacy." And then she slapped her leg and laughed her gutsy laugh at her own waggishness. I was tempted to say, "Don't put a pink rose in it, for it stands for grace and beauty," but I put my temptation behind me and reined my tongue.

Just as Liz was about to discard the leaves she had stripped off, Mrs. Potts restrained her. "I'll put some of these in the mutton stew I'm making from yesterday's haunch. Remember, girl, 'Waste not, want not'!" Following Cook's example, I said I'd take the ones Cook did not need for my surprise for Mother.

I must admit I am disappointed to learn Clive is to be Daisy's husband. I look on him as one of my best friends, and I don't want to lose my friend. And once he is married, I guess we can no longer be friends. At least it won't be the same.

Upon reflection, I realize that Clive has never revealed anything of a personal nature about himself to me. But then he is not a person of words.

As I am writing I hear the call of the cuckoo bird coming from the garden. Back before Nanny became so deaf she would put lamb's wool in her ears, because she said that incessant cry could drive a person cuckoo. To me it sounds like the lonely bird is calling for a mate. It may not make one of unsound mind, but it does keep one from falling asleep.

Dear Diary,

The sun is shining but it's still a grey day to me.

On our way to services, as we passed the kitchen, I heard sounds of someone crying emanating from the scullery. As I peered in I saw Liz with her face buried in her hands trying to stifle her sobs. I went to her and finally pried from her that Daisy had returned to the village, but Clive had been arrested with charges that he had stolen Thunder. Liz asserted that he had only borrowed Thunder and intended to return him, but the horse had run away from them on their way. When Lord Lyon's man came for his horse and learned that Clive had taken him, he had pursued and apprehended Clive before the couple reached Gretna Green. Though I tried to comfort her, telling her that Papa would fix everything when he returns, she was inconsolable. She said the hearing will be held tomorrow, not in our village but in Hereford where the assizes are in session to try serious crimes like stealing a horse. The magistrates who preside come only quarterly, and will be strangers to Clive. I tried to assure her that when they learn he was only borrowing the horse they would understand. She protested that she is told that the person accused of the crime cannot take the stand in his own defense. And as Clive is no longer a boy who might be sentenced to receive only a public whipping, and as the stealing of a horse is too serious to be sentenced only a few weeks in the bridewell, she has fear that he will be sentenced to a public hanging. Between great wails and sobs she said that all the parents in the village would bring their children, especially young girls, so that they will see the consequence of sinful behaviour. It was then that she confessed that Daisy is with child, and that that is why they were eloping. She burst into tears, lamenting that her whole family is disgraced and that it would be the ruin of her because she will never find a husband now.

I must confess I was shocked by this revelation. How could two people forget what is due to common sense and propriety? How could Clive, indeed anyone, indulge in such irresponsible behaviour, which would reflect not only on the poor baby but everyone in his family as well as Daisy's?

Maggie was in the kitchen taking a cup of tea and offered to read the leaves left in Liz's teacup. She took the cup and gently turned it about in order to read the symbols without disturbing them. The scattered leaves formed lines and circles of dots, which meant nothing to me. Maggie pointed out that the groupings were in the shapes of triangles, stars, or clover leaves, which indicated good luck; others like an hourglass, an umbrella, or an owl were omens of bad luck. But, she assured Liz, the good omens outweighed the bad ones! And here she said was an angel, which means good fortune in matters of love. Maggie declared that she saw a bridge indicating a favourable journey and a chain suggesting an early marriage, and as these signs were located near the rim of the cup, they were more likely to happen in the near future.

I was peering over her shoulder the whole time and try as I would, it was still meaningless confusion to me.

I do not think that Maggie believed anything she said. I think she simply wanted to comfort Liz.

Today at church services I prayed very hard for Clive's life. I'm sure God understood that was more important than the sermon.

I wish Mr. Austin-Brown were here. I wish Papa were here. Maybe even Cousin Hubert could be of some help if he were here. He could plead Clive's case and I would think that the Justices would be impressed with Cousin Hubert's distinguished oratory.

After services I went into the kitchen to comfort Liz, but she had gone to the village. Cook was dozing by the hearth in her rocking chair, her pudgy hands, like unkneaded dough, clasped over her fat stomach. Her ample bosom rose and fell with each whistling snore. So I tiptoed on to the garden to take advantage of the sunshine with my sketching. My mind was troubled and, instead of sketching the foxgloves as I intended, I found myself trying to draw Thunder.

I wondered how I would feel if my dearest, sweetest Bess was stolen from me. But to kill the thief! Is the theft of an animal worth the life of a man? One of the Ten Commandments is "Thou shalt not kill." How can Christians justify hanging a man?

I fear Papa will never let Clive return because of his shameful behaviour, but I know he would not want Clive to be hanged. If only the assizes was not already in session I'm sure Papa could fix everything.

Even though I am afraid we can no longer be friends, I will pray tonight for Clive's life.

Thunder

Dear Diary,

Thunder has been found and returned to our stables. It will be a few days before Lord Lyon can return for him. I asked Bridget to come with me to the stable to see if Thunder's experience has made him all nervy again.

When we passed the barnyard a pullet was squawking loudly because Liz had just caught her. Suddenly Liz swung the chicken around and around, holding only to her head. The head came off in her hand, and the headless bird ran helter-skelter around the barnyard. I found it disturbing to see the muscles of the headless creature still functioning. I wondered if the brain was still thinking, and if it was feeling pain. I said to Bridget that I didn't think I could ever kill a chicken.

Bridget looked thoughtful and then said, "I don't suppose you've ever been hungry." Bridget's naturally florid complexion then coloured even more deeply crimson, and she said, "I'll tell you one thing I'd never do. Some of the boys at home would take a rooster by his feet and swing him around and around over their heads, because when they released the poor bird he would stagger around as if it was drunk. Then they would laugh their heads off. I'd never take advantage of a helpless creature like that." I liked her for that.

By now Liz had dipped the headless carcass in a pot of boiling water and was plucking off the feathers. Bridget offered to help her, but I found the odour so distasteful that I insisted we must proceed to the stable.

On the way we stopped by the walled kitchen garden to pick a carrot for Bess. To my surprise the gate was open. Thomas came shuffling out with his toes turned out in a most ungainly gait. He had a scowl on his face, and a poor dead bunny hanging limp from his hoe. The churlish man was muttering to himself that it was a wonder the deer had not gotten in and eaten all of his tenderest plants. He had bludgeoned the poor little creature to death and all the bunny had done was to feed himself. I know the bunny didn't realize he was doing anything wrong. Now Thomas was placing blame on one of his helpers and was off to give him some lashes, I fear.

I've been thinking. Rabbits don't kill anything. Foxes eat rabbits and chickens, and hounds eat the foxes. Chickens eat insects and worms, and people eat not only chickens but sheep and cattle and deer. Big fish eat little fish—sometimes their own babies. I commented to Bridget that I couldn't understand how a good God could let this happen. She answered, "Not everything that happens in the world is caused by God. I don't think we should worry about it. It's best that we take what happens and use it to develop as spiritual persons. God will take care of everything, and sooner or later all will work out in the right direction." Bridget may not do well with her letters, but she does quite well with her thoughts.

Thunder was a bit skittish, but nothing like he was when Papa first brought him to our stables. I think he is happy to be back in his box.

When we returned from the stable, I heard Liz singing a happy ditty! She rushed to tell me she'd received word that the trial had been held and God had answered our prayers. The Judges had even intervened to query Clive, and the jury fortunately included a man who knew Clive's family. After much deliberation, it found him guilty of stealing only a bridle, saying the horse just followed along because the bridle was fastened around its head. Instead of being sent to a gaol where he would be held with hardened criminals, or being transported to Australia, he was sentenced to do public work crushing rocks for mending roadways. And now Daisy's parents are giving their permission for their marriage, so that their baby will be legitimate after all. I wonder how Papa will feel about all this, and if Papa will send Clive away. I know that Papa would never condone such irresponsible, sinful behaviour, but now that they are to be married perhaps he will let Clive stay.

Dear Diary,

Feeling a pang of shame at my negligence, I spent the morning in endeavour to improve my mastery of the pianoforte. I know that when Mother and Father return they will ask me to perform for them and my hand at the piano is definitely not fine. I like to sing songs and hear other people play, but I fear I own a dislike of practice. In fact, I confess I detest doing my scales. To make it less tedious, sometimes I play them slowly and sometimes fast, sometimes staccato and sometimes with pedal.

Nanny says,

> *"Good, better, best*
> *Never rest*
> *Till good be better and*
> *Better best."*

And she has told me many times, "It's better to fail well than to succeed badly," so I guess I must keep trying. Mother plays expertly, and her hands look beautiful gliding up and down the keys. I fear I must be a trial to her, because at piano, at penmanship, and at needlework I do not excel.

After our midday meal, Bridget and I worked together to master her alphabet. Bridget does not lack the wit to understand, nor memory to remember. More important, she is eager to learn. However, I fear her progress will require more time began to think he was but a figment of my imagination. Then I decided he must be a gypsy. But then I heard a violent thrashing of the undergrowth, with a snapping of branches, and I could see a hulking shaggy figure passing through the shadows. It looked like a bear, but then I told myself we have no wild bears in England. I wanted to turn and run, but I felt as if my feet were of lead and I was unable to move them. Cold shivers ran down my spine.

A large man with a straggly beard, his clothing dirty and disheveled, his eyes bloodshot and bleary, staggered onto the path directly in front of me but stopped abruptly when he saw me. He was carrying a substantial stick. He was so close I could smell the offensive odor of his unwashed body.

"Where did he go?" he demanded.

I'd never had anyone in his station address me in this way. I was filled with trepidation for fear that he would do me mischief. I drew myself up as tall as I could.

"The little fox ran across my path just now, and into the wood on the other side."

His unfocused eyes looked suspiciously down at me. "I meant my son, of course," he said with blurred words, and then, as if the way I was dressed made him suddenly realize to whom he was speaking, he added, "M'lady."

Only then did I realize that those porcine eyes belonged to Tenant Swinert.

"I've had a lookout for the doe with the twin fawns but

haven't spied them. Have you seen them?" I asked. (To this he had no answer but stared at me blankly.) What else I said, I do not now know, but I prattled on to give the poor lad time to escape. His breath was heavy and he grunted something unintelligible, hesitated, and then turned and headed back whence he had come.

I had controlled my shaking by the time I reached the house. I wanted to tell someone what had happened, but I dared not tell Nanny, for I did not want the unfortunate boy to get in trouble.

I will certainly report this to Papa upon his return. Papa has been gone twenty-six days and surely will return soon, as that is much more than a fortnight.

Dear Diary,

It was such a beautiful day that I invited Bridget to join me on a ramble around the grounds as soon as she could complete her duties. As we walked about the gardens she stopped at each vista, as if awed by the sight. "Oh! It's beautiful! So different from Ireland. Getting to know this land is like discovering a new friend." I had seen what she viewed many times, but through her eyes it was with new appreciation. The sun was gilding the tops of the trees fringing the lakes. The fields were lush with red clover. The crop in the field spread a carpet of gold, and the sky was of the tenderest blue, a colour I've never been able to duplicate with my watercolours.

I realized how much the Primrose land means to me. It is a familiar but always an interesting friend. It changes constantly—with the weather, the seasons, even the time of day.

I offered to show Bridget the grotto. As we walked down the path that wound through the treillages covered in honeysuckle, our nostrils filled with the sweetness of the flowers, our ears with the hum of bees, and the happy spattering of water on the stones of the brook in the water garden.

We stopped to watch a small bird perched on a rock, dipping and bobbing in the manner characteristic of a water ousel. Bridget thought I was joshing her when I told her that water ousels walk on the bottom of the stream to feed. She was not convinced until the little bird dipped into the water and disappeared for a period of time, finally emerging on the opposite side of the stream.

When I disclosed to Bridget that the entrance to the grotto could be achieved only by walking on the stepping-stones in the stream and ducking under the waterfall, she protested that she was no water ousel and revealed that she did not know how to swim. I offered to hold her hand and she was reassured. But then when we entered the dark, damp, long low-ceilinged tunnel, the atmosphere seemed stagnant and humid. I explained that the tunnel leads to the hermit's chamber, and Bridget anxiously protested that this is just such a place as the "little people" inhabit. She felt we needed to stop to say a charm or half a spell to prevent them from changing shape or playing tricks on us. I assured her that we have no "little people" in England, and in fact no longer even have a hermit in our grotto.

Great-grandfather, who had built the tunnel to the grotto, had given sanctuary to a hermit because he felt the hermit added atmosphere, but since the hermit died, the grotto has been used solely as entertainment for guests. I explained that the chamber originally was a natural cave in the hillside and opens to the lake, where a large rock serves as a dock for a boat. In Grandfather's library there are strange chiseled stones retrieved from it, said to be from the days of ancient peoples called Druids. This thought adds a mysterious aura to the grotto, and I always hope to stumble onto some prehistoric item when I visit it. Mother tells me that I have French, Celtic, and Roman blood. I wonder if I have Druid blood as well. Whatever happened to those long-ago people? Did they all die of some plague, or were they killed by the Celts when they came? I asked Bridget if she had Druid blood, but she had never heard of Druids. I had hoped that we could both have the same blood in our veins.

We proceeded down the tunnel in the dark, but the chamber itself is lighted from a crevice in the ceiling. When we arrived at the chamber it took a few minutes for our eyes to adjust to the light. I felt Bridget stiffen and halt. Just as I was about to lose patience with her superstitious notions I detected a light object moving in the darkest corner of the chamber, and indeed a figure crossed my line of vision, as short as if it were one of the "little people." Bridget and I were about to turn and run back down the passage when a small voice spoke haltingly. "Excuse me, M'lady, for being here."

It was my playmate of old, Tenant Swinert's son, Lettuce. I then realized it was he who had run past me in the woods yesterday. Though near my age he is much shorter than I am; he seems to have stopped growing. Assured that he wasn't a ghost or one of Bridget's "little people," I asked him why he was here.

Stuttering, he explained that he had lost his employment at the pot house in the village because he was not artistic. He was afraid to return home because his father would beat him. I tried to assure him that it was not his fault, and that surely his father would understand, but he simply shook his head and said, as if he knew whereof he spoke, "He has already boxed my ears. Now he will beat me." It was then that I noticed the bruises on his face and his blackened eye. This distressed me, and I felt I should let him stay in the grotto until Papa returned and even have Liz bring him food.

To my surprise Bridget spoke up. "Perhaps you can find other employment, if not in the village, perhaps in one of the larger towns." I remembered Papa talking about the new textile mills soon to open, so I told Lettuce about them. And then I thought of the coal mines I had read about in Papa's paper. They like small people because the tunnels are so small. I explained to him that the government had recently made a law that children under twelve cannot work in the mines, for though small, Lettuce is of a sufficient age. His face looked drawn and sad as he apologized again for startling us. When he left his shoulders were drooping, his pale pinched face the picture of despair.

On our way back to the Hall I spoke of a nagging concern to Bridget. Should we have advised him to leave his family? His mother and brothers and sisters are his family, too. Don't they need him?

She replied that she did not think he could help them by staying there and taking his father's abuse. Hopefully he could earn enough to enable some of his brothers and sisters or even his mother to escape their degradation.

I dare not tell Nanny or anyone, for fear of getting the lad in trouble. My heart is sorely concerned. I prayed that his father would not beat him. I wish Papa would return home soon. I'm sure he'd make everything right.

I received a letter from Papa today. It was so welcome I didn't immediately break the seal, but held it close to my heart relishing the anticipation of reading it.

Once opened, I read and reread it imagining myself in London. I'm sure Papa and Mother will take me with them someday.

Dear Cygnet,

Today your mother and I called for the equipage and went to Chelsea to attend services at St. Luke's Church because we wished to hear the Reverend Charles Kingsley. Though not yet thirty years old, he delivered a most thought-provoking sermon. The essence was that to fully understand the meaning of a Father in Heaven we must be fathers ourselves. To know how Christ loved the Church, we must have wives and love them. Mother especially appreciated that part of the sermon. After services we engaged in an interesting discourse with him. He told us he is working on a symbolic book for children, which he plans to title The Water Babies. In the book, Tom, a young chimney sweep, will by magical transformation by fairies, be washed clean and turned into a water baby, and find happiness and spiritual redemption through the creatures he befriends in his watery world. It impresses me that Reverend Kingsley will spend his efforts to make his messages understood by children.

Your Mother and I had planned to go to the Chelsea Physic Garden, where she buys her medicinal plants every year. She especially wants to procure feverfew and sweet marjoram plants, as she has been told both may be helpful with the aches in her head. The Apothecaries Company founded it nearly seventy-five years ago. Your Great-grandfather, who originally planted our herb garden, used to buy his plants there. Since Mother was feeling ill we postponed the visit and strolled the garden on the south side of the church, and then down the elm _allée_ in the garden of the Royal Hospital.

On our return we ordered the coachman to drive to the East India docks near Brunswick so that we could view the Royal Chinese junk which keyed from Canton, China. I read that Her Royal Highness and Prince Albert expressed great admiration for it. As we neared the Thames the unpleasant odour of dead fish was overwhelming, so we satisfied ourselves with a dockside look.

I wished for your grandfather on our return to the house. As we traversed Lower Thomas Street we passed the ruins of a Roman villa discovered last February during excavation for a new building. With his love of antiquities, he would have been most interested.

We have been invited to dinner next week by the Duke of Wellington at Apsley House, which boasts one of the largest dining rooms in London. Even though Parliament is not in session, there will be a large group attending—possibly, I hope, even Lord Russell, our Prime Minister. I wish to express my admiration for his leadership last year in the passage of legislation limiting working hours in factories. In addition, he is responsible for the passing of the Public Health Act this year. Boards are now being established to see that new homes have proper drainage and clean local water supplies. They will supervise also the construction of burial grounds much needed, as most graveyards have been long since filled.

Your mother is hoping our meal will be served on the Sèvres

Egyptian Service commissioned by Napoleon for his Empress Josephine.

We will be returning soon. I am always happy to return home to Primrose Hall and you and William.

Mother sends her tidings to all in the household. At her request, I am enclosing a receipt for a toothing syrup and ask you to please have Cook to mix it and send it over to Mrs. Swinert for her baby boy.

Your ever affectionate
Papa

Toothing Syrup for Children
Take Syrup of Buckthorne 2 Dr
of Syrup of Saffron —— 1 Dr
of Syrup of Violetts —— 1 Dr
of Syrup of Rohenbart - 1/2 Oz
Mix. A Teaspoonfule of this mix
to be given to the Child twice
a Day & a little rubbed on the
Gums ——

Dear Diary,

It is overcast this morning. It may be a dreadfully dull day.

Yesterday Nanny discovered that William appeared fever-ish. At first she assumed his recent stressful situation could be the cause. But later in the day he appeared to have broken out with the pox that Nanny assures me must be chicken pox. I wonder if one gets chicken pox from chickens. I know that one gets cowpox from cows and it's good to have it, because if you do, then you won't get smallpox. In my evening prayers I will thank God that William has chicken pox and not smallpox.

I do hope Nanny has made no mistake. I feel great respon-sibility and contrition for William's condition. There was our visit to the henhouse and then the near accident in the cel-larette. I could not bear it if William has succumbed to the dreadful scourge.

Nanny has declared that he must remain in the nursery chambers and I am not to visit him, as though I have had cow-pox and measles and whooping cough, I have never had the chicken pox.

To soothe the itching, Bridget brought up a lotion, which Cook had prepared by steeping dried marigold petals and rose-mary leaves in water. I could think of nothing I could do for him, so I had Bridget wait while I wrote a conundrum for Nanny to read to him. "Why is a cistern like one of the great seas?"—Because it's Made to Rain In! I hope William remembers our lesson on the Mediterranean.

Bridget didn't know about this ocean and I promised to take her to Grandfather's library and show her on his globe of the world.

Later

The sun has broken through the clouds. It is now a brilliant day—so warm and sunny. Mr. Austin-Brown has finally returned!

He brought me a present from a distant cousin, a lady who recently returned from studying art in Paris—instructions for painting on glass and for making a watercolour look like an oil painting. I wondered if his cousin was pretty and if she was the reason he was gone for so many days.

Without William, lessons were more interesting than ever. To my surprise Mr. Austin-Brown didn't scold me for not completing his assignments, which made me feel more contrite than if he had done so.

After lessons I stayed in the schoolroom to engage Mr. Austin-Brown in conversation. The quickness of his mind expresses itself in the fluency of his utterances. I was glad for the moment that William was indisposed and not able to interrupt. Mr. Austin-Brown asked me if I'd like him to teach me Latin. When I seemed hesitant, he said, "You are too intelligent to fritter your life away with silly trifles! Even if you never mastered Latin well enough to read Virgil you would still find it helpful, as so many of our words of today are derived from Latin." Though I have never before thought I would be able to learn Greek or Latin, I think I would enjoy learning them from Mr. Austin-Brown. He always makes any lesson interesting. And he said I was intelligent!

Mr. Austin-Brown seems greatly discouraged. He said that he had been accepted at King's College, but there were no scholarship funds available for him. I could think of nothing to say that would alleviate his disappointment. I wanted to lay my hand on his in comfort, but I did not have the courage to do so.

I ran to my room and brought my pen-and-ink-enhanced drawings. He said he thought they were excellent, the ink greatly improving my sketches. I vowed that I would be more diligent in my artistic endeavours.

After the noon meal Bridget and I went to the stables to see Bess and Thunder. Thunder seems totally happy to be back in his stall. On our return I picked some walnuts, still in their green casings, from a low hanging branch of the walnut tree. I planned to make a boat for William out of the shell, with a twig for the mast and a leaf for the sail. When I tried to peel the casing off it was too green, and all I succeeded in doing was staining my fingers indelibly brown. Abandoning that idea, I decided to make a nosegay of the deep blue Michaelmas daisies growing wild along the path. I will give it to him tomorrow because it will be Michaelmas Day.

On our return to the house, we pursued our way down the lane leading to the entrance gate. I gathered some moss because I decided to make a Lilliputian garden in a biscuit tin for William. He can use it for one of his beetles. A flash of colour caught my eye as we neared the entrance gates. At first I thought it was the tinker with his colourful cart of wares and hastened in order to tell him that Cook needs a new copper to heat our water. It proved to be one of the gypsy women, who stopped when she saw us approaching. In spite of her swarthy complexion, she had a not-unattractive appearance. Her eyes were dark, and she wore hoops in her ears, and a bright red riband tied back her shoulder-length black hair.

She asked if I would like her to read my palm and foretell my future. I felt in my pocket and the coin was still there. I drew it out and showed it to her and said I would if she would read Bridget's future, too. She hesitated, but deducing that I only had the one coin and that I would not engage her if she did not read both our destinies, she nodded yes.

Taking Bridget's hand, she ran her finger along the lines of Bridget's palm. I noticed that the gypsy's hand was soiled and she had dirt under her fingernail. She studied the lines and said that Bridget would receive news of a serious nature that would occasion her to cross deep waters. Then she said she

Dearest Little Cygnet,

I had a leisurely morning in my study attending to my correspondence and reading the <u>Morning Post</u>. One of the delights of
being in the city is being current on the events.

Employment is up in the manufacturing districts, the bank-
ing panic is being blamed on the government's Bank Restructure
policy of just four years ago, and there is talk that the Direc-
tors may relax the conditions of the Bank Charter. The agita-
tion of stocks is being blamed upon all the political upheaval
in France, Germany, and Italy.

In Ireland, aggravated by the harangues of some of the priest-
hood, atrocious crimes, assassinations, and robberies against any
landholder were rampant last spring. Some of the perpetrators
have already faced trial and been handed out justice. Bridget
can be thankful that her father is a glazier.

The <u>Illustrated London News</u> reports that the arrival in
Dublin of our Prime Minister Lord Russell, accompanied by his
Lady, was met with only faint cheers but at least did not get
up a groan. It is reported that His Lordship has accepted an
invitation from the Earl of Charlesmont to spend a few days at
his beautiful residence near Clontarf.

Then in the very same column a letter from a priest in
Ireland reports the cruel and heartless eviction of some of
the Irish people, throwing their houses to the ground and leaving fifty-four souls homeless as well as starving. I hope

Lord Russell will address these misfortunes as well as enjoy himself.

I feel disgusted with the ills of society, the violence, the corruption.

One might wish to stick his head in the sand like an ostrich, but one must interest oneself in these matters. If problems are not addressed they can become disasters. One does what one can do on a personal basis to materially relieve distressful conditions, but frequently it takes effort by a community of people or even, as a last resort, governmental action. I have had no ambition to stand for a seat in Parliament, knowing that high office cannot buy happiness. However, I am beginning to feel it is my duty as a citizen of our great Empire and as a Christian.

Baron Rothschild was admitted as a new member of Parliament in spite of the fact he said that he could not in good faith take the prescribed oath: "on the true faith of a Christian." He seems to be a man of good heart even if he is not a Christian. Governance cannot be entrusted to men who have no ideals.

Always live up to your highest ideals, Cygnet. A life without principles is not worth living. Grow in love for your country and its heritage of manners, virtues, and laws. In our loyal obedience to Our Lord, our reason, and our conscience lies our highest liberty. You will find that integrity is a gift to yourself. I enclose a poem I felt moved to compose for you.

Much of this letter may be of little interest to you, dear child, so share this news with the other members of our house-

hold. They will take pleasure in the fact that they are more current on the news of the city than anyone within miles.

Your Mother would write but she has not been feeling well today.

Help Nanny to take care of William.

Your loving
Papa

TRUTH IN US

Your wish and will to serve
The truth the life and the way
The Perfect One who came before—
Perhaps the virtue then is more
Action—the doing—the knowing
Setting the course and rowing
Steadily with heart and hope
Aware that He is with you
Watching wind, current and stars
Over obstacles, channels and bars.

Winning is living the Word
Solomon was wise, have you heard
His concise expressions of wisdom?
Can you challenge any?
Can you improve on truth?

The directions to some say
"When truth fails, slip away."
This won't work at all
The truth—truth is the wall
Within a positive confident place
Outside only discomfort and disgrace.

Can you tell when you're there?
Is it contrivable, do you care?
Does honesty dwell in you?
Will others police what you do?
Food for thought in each station—
Truth and respect can build our Nation.

—William Godfrey Primrose
September 26, 1848

Dear Diary,

My geography lesson today was about India, the source of our tea and so many other products since it is part of our British Empire. Mr. Austin-Brown talked about how the natives regard all animals, like monkeys and cows, as sacred, even though the elephants are trained to work moving big logs. He described the tigers, which he said can kill people. William is still confined to his room. I knew that William would have especially liked Mr. Austin-Brown's description of the tigers, and I almost wished he could be here.

But with no interruptions from William it was a wonderful day. Latin is not as difficult as I had anticipated. Mr. Austin-Brown is very encouraging and has clever suggestions for remembering vocabulary. After lessons he seemed in no hurry to leave. We talked a long time and not about lessons.

When I told him of my concern over the advice Bridget and I had given to Lettuce, he reassured me, saying that there comes a time when a person must depend upon himself. His face became solemn and sad, and he confided, "I have been on my own since I was fourteen."

Speaking hesitantly, he told me that six years ago his entire family—his father, his mother, his three little sisters—were all killed when their home caught fire and burned to the ground. He was the only member of his family left, as he had departed the previous day to return to his school, Rugby. Though there was no one to pay the balance of his tuition, because his father had been a Master there he was allowed to stay until graduation.

He brushed his hand across his eyes and wiped away the tears brimming there. Pausing a minute, he then spoke in a voice full of resolution.

"Since that day I have pondered why God spared me and what He wishes me to do with my life. I had always wanted to be a poet but I recently came to the realisation that such a profound art takes more than adroitness with words and a sense of rhythm.

"I have come to believe that it is God's Will that I read history at Cambridge. Without knowledge of the past one cannot appreciate the present, or understand what the future may hold. Only with the wisdom knowledge can bring can I use my passion for poetry for the good of others."

I told him that when I read poetry I have to slow down and really think about what I am reading. I then look into it and not just at it. People enjoy poetry so much that it is an excellent way to convey his thoughts.

To think I'd known him all these months and had never known his heart this way! What a selfish person I am. I have been thinking only of myself and never inquired about his life. He must miss his family as much as I miss Dearest Sister and

Grandfather. I feel ashamed that I so resented his wanting to leave and attend King's College. I wonder: "Why did God take Dearest Sister and leave me?"

I wanted to converse longer, but he rose and declared that Cook would be peeved with him if he was late for his midday meal. Then I hurried through my meal with Nanny so that I could take a turn around the park on Thunder. I am determined to ride him at least once before Lord Lyon takes him away.

Once at the stable, I found that Tom was out exercising the horses. With Clive gone, I decided to saddle Thunder myself and ride him around the paddock. To be certain that Thunder trusted me, I stroked his forehead and scratched him behind the ears. He allowed me to saddle him and stood still so that he could be mounted with ease. Bess, looking over the half door to her stall, whinnied when I rode past her box, and I felt a pang of guilt. Thunder was calm and responsive to the lightest hand.

Riding in the paddock soon became tiresome. I decided to open the gate and take a turn about the park. Once outside the paddock I found Thunder had a mind of his own. With an exceedingly rapid pace he headed straight for the orchard, and once there started eating the fruit from the apple trees. He continued to munch away happily, no matter how much I kicked his flanks or pulled on the reins. I was afraid he'd eat so many apples Mrs. Potts would be angry with me, for it takes a lot of apples to make our cider vinegar and apple butter.

The beehives are in the orchard as well, and in his eager-
ness Thunder knocked over one of the hives and the upset
bees filled the air.

Suddenly Thunder reared. I clung to the saddle as tightly as
possible, for now he needed no urging. At full gallop we
headed down the narrow lane toward the stable. I tried to rein
him in to no avail. Terrified that I would fall, I concentrated on
keeping my seat.

Mr. Austin-Brown, who was walking to his quarters, saw
us coming. He stopped and stood in the middle of the narrow
lane, waving his hands above his head to stop the runaway animal. The out-of-control horse thundered on, with Mr. Austin-
Brown directly in his path. I suddenly feared for Mr.
Austin-Brown's safety as well as my own. Thunder exhibited
no sign of slowing down, but Mr. Austin-Brown bravely did
not retreat and continued waving his hands.

Just as we reached him, Thunder, being a hunter, took the
hedge, and off I fell into the arms of Mr. Austin-Brown,
knocking him to the ground with me on top of him, my petti-
coats over my head. I was embarrassed at the impropriety of
being in such an unladylike position. With difficulty, we both
scrambled to our feet. Tom, who had witnessed the mishap
from the stable, came running.

Mr. Austin-Brown, after assuring himself that I had no serious injury, looked me in the face as if he had never seen me
before. I was so ruffled that I fear my face was suffused with

scarlet. He then exclaimed that a bee seemed to have bitten me on the face, and that bees must have bitten Thunder as well, explaining the cause of his wild actions. I was very embarrassed to have anyone think that I could not control my mount, so I felt great relief that there was an excuse for my lack of horsemanship.

Tom suggested that I come to the stables so he could apply hartshorn to my beesting, but my leg was hurt from the fall. Mr. Austin-Brown assured him that we would stop by the kitchen and make a paste from carbonate of soda that would relieve the pain.

Mr. Austin-Brown's face was filled with concern. As I was limping, he walked back to the house with me, with his arm around my waist to help support me. His shoulders seemed very broad, and the muscles in his arm very strong. I think I could have walked without support but I didn't protest so. I was sorry when we reached the house.

To make me feel better he said, "I think they gave Thunder the wrong name—he should have been named Lightning." We laughed together, and the laugh made me forget the pain.

His expression, usually so serious, was more animated than I'd ever seen it. His sensitive face was much more handsome than I'd taken note of previously. His eyes twinkled, their irises larger than ever.

With Mr. Austin-Brown so close to me, the odour of his witch hazel made me think of Papa. I remembered Papa's face when the dancing master put his arm around Mother's waist. I knew he would not have approved if he had seen me and Mr. Austin-Brown walking. And I should not have ridden Thunder without Papa's permission.

Mr. Austin-Brown didn't mention to Nanny what had occurred, and I felt very thankful to him.

My beesting did not swell at all. And my hurt leg walks perfectly firm now. I should have told Mr. Austin-Brown that I did not need his help walking, but I did not. I don't know why but I keep feeling Mr. Austin-Brown's arm around my waist— and it is strange, but I like it.

Dear Diary,

Last evening before I went to bed I was looking out the window, listening to the fiddling of the crickets and watching the fireflies when I saw Tobias crouching low and stalking something near the root cellar. He may be a good mouser, but he provides no satisfaction as a pet. He will not even allow me to approach him; in fact, the only time I was ever near him he scratched my face. I thought about Mr. Blake's poem in one of Grandfather's books, which I liked so much that I read and reread it until I knew it by memory.

> Tyger! Tyger! burning bright
> In the forests of the night,
> What immortal hand or eye
> Could frame thy fearful symmetry?

During the night I had a dream that a huge fierce tiger of vivid orange and black was crouching low and stalking me through the grove. His eyes were gleaming as green as bottles with the sunlight shining through them. I tried to run fast but I couldn't seem to move. Suddenly the tiger's face looked like Tenant Swinert's. And then I saw our church with the doors opened wide. I ran down the aisle towards the altar. The angel from Dearest Sister's grave was there with her arms outstretched to receive me. At that point I was no longer afraid and I awakened. There was Tobias crouching on my windowsill, his eyes gleaming in the dark.

Perhaps Nanny is right about not opening the windows in our bedchamber.

Later

After lessons this morning I told Mr. Austin-Brown about my dreaming about a tiger, and he asked me if the dream was in colour. When I said it was he took my hand, looked me in the eyes, and said, "That means that you are artistic. Most people do not dream in colour, you know."

I'd never noticed that his eyes, so clear, are as amber as the brandy in Papa's decanter. I felt strange to have him holding my hand. I stared at my hand, which seemed so small in his large one. His fingers were strong, yet long and slender. I could not quell the flutter of my heart, and I worried that he could hear it. I hoped that he didn't find my stained fingers displeasing. He continued to hold my hand, as if he had forgotten he was doing so. Finally he released it, and then fell back into his old manner. "And that means you must express yourself in creative ways. Never execute your sketches with indifference and be diligent with your writing. You know that writing is like painting with words. You can use your creativity to transform your life into life for others."

He then dug into his pocket and drew forth a folded paper. "I've written the poem I promised you," he said, and he proceeded to read it. I was hypnotized by the fall of the words upon my ears. I could scarcely believe he was referring to me. It was most kind indeed. Of course, it was exaggeration, especially the curly ringlet part. I wonder if he knows I roll my hair in rags every night. He then gave it to me. With the most diligent care I shall always keep it, a memory like a flower pressed between the pages of a book.

I resolved that I would be conscientious in my future

artistic endeavours. I can still feel the warmth of his hand clasping my hand. It is a good feeling and I like it very much. I like Mr. Austin-Brown very much.

> A Diana with her book the bow
> Captures with pen rather than arrow
>
> Her inquisitive mind never at rest
> Searching always for understanding best
>
> A visage so handsome and fair
> Her presence perfumes the air
>
> Ringlets blond about her face
> Every movement filled with grace
>
> Her sparkling eyes clear and blue
> Delight at each idea novel and new
>
> Her dimpled cheeks pink with pleasure
> Her deepest essence so hard to measure.
>
> —John Austin-Brown
> September 29, 1848

would be embarrassed if they thought I was watching them, so I turned on my heel and headed for the stable.

There was my sweetest, dearest Bess, always glad to see me. She nuzzled me with her soft nose. I hugged her neck and then curried her until I felt better before I returned to my chamber. When I returned Nanny told me that Bridget had been looking for me to work on her letters, and I felt remorse for my silliness. I tried to read the book assignment Mr. Austin-Brown had given me, but though I read the words the meaning escaped me.

I finally gave up and got out Papa's letters and read and re-read them. I cannot sleep because of the lonely cry of the cuckoo bird.

Dear Diary,

I was early for my lessons this morning, for once. Mr. Austin-Brown rushed into the schoolroom today in a state of great excitement, his face flushed with pleasure. His mind was rushing so that his words had difficulty keeping up, but the quickness of his wits could be seen on his face. "Today's lesson is our last!" he exclaimed in a most lively voice. "I relied on providence and have been rewarded! An unknown benefactor has volunteered to fund me. I have now the means to become a sizar at King's College, and I can devote myself to the study of history and writing my poetry. I consider it my calling. A study of history gives one humility, and yet at the same time audacity. And then I hope to express my understanding in my poetry for all posterity."

A lock of his abundant chestnut hair had fallen over his brow. The demeanour of his earnest face with eyes full of fire had never seemed so fair. There was a youthful wildness, yet a thoughtful expression, in his countenance.

As he wishes to matriculate for the Michaelmas term he must depart as soon as possible. He stayed with our lessons for the full time, even giving me extra time on my Latin lesson. I wanted the lesson never to end, but finally he said he must go to gather his belongings. He gave me his Latin book, and to please him I promised I would continue with the endeavour—though I fear I lack the discipline to do so.

In spite of the efforts of all my will I find it most difficult to share in Mr. Austin-Brown's happiness at his good fortune. Now I shall never learn Latin, and I shall sorely miss our time together. Mr. Austin-Brown was a strong taskmaster but always fair. Remnants of the happy times we spent in the schoolroom settled around my heart like dust, and I knew that they were never to be made whole again.

Dear Diary,

It was a blue, slate blue day. Mr. Austin-Brown left today for Cambridge. In the realization that I might never see him again, I was sufficiently forward to ask him to send me his address so that I might write him a letter. He took my hand between his, his wide-set eyes looked me in the eyes, and he promised to write. His voice was deep and resonant, yet gentle. A shadow of sadness briefly passed over his countenance, but the excitement of his new life soon filled his attentions. When he withdrew his hand, I felt as if he was taking my heart with it.

There was scarcely room for him on his conveyance, as it was piled high with boxes of his books, his lap desk, his portmanteau, and even his fencing foil. I stood at the door of the Hall and watched until it was out of sight.

Nanny declared with a snort, "Well, there he goes with his pipe dreams. If he continues his pursuit of poetry, he could give his whole heart and soul for bare maintenance and hardly that." I started to tell her that Grandfather's friends Mr. Coleridge and Mr. Wordsworth are poets and surely they earn more than bare maintenance, but I decided to refrain from retort.

Then Nanny remarked what a generous act it was for Papa to make it possible for him to become one of the sizars. I couldn't understand what she meant. What did Papa have to do with it?

She said she thought I must have known that Papa was his unknown benefactor. I was speechless. I did not know what to think. I could not imagine why Papa would take away the only good tutor I ever had. I felt a crushing sadness. She then added that Papa will no doubt find a new tutor at the school the government has recently established in London to train governesses. This I did not find at all reassuring.

I remember my last tutor, Mlle. Alice, who, though fair of face, was a frivolous woman of vapid intelligence. She gave herself airs and insisted she be called Mademoiselle, even though she was as English as I was. She could speak French very well, having lived in France for a year. She made me hate French. When I protested to Nanny that Mademoiselle was a silly goose, Nanny reprimanded me, saying, "If you can't say something nice, don't say anything at all!" But I knew she didn't like her either. In fact, I heard her complain to Cook that all the insipid woman thought about was a certain dragoon guardsman with a dyed, waxed mustache, who was probably a rake and only trifling with her affections. Nanny told Cook she read to Mlle. Alice from her latest issue of <u>Family Friend</u>: "Before you marry, be sure of a house wherein to tarry." All she got from her was a tart reply in French, spoken so fast that she knew Nanny would not be able to understand her.

Sudden fear struck my heart! Surely Papa would not send me to one of those terrible academies for young females, which only teach social graces, piano, and needlework and won't even give you candles by which to read. I find it wasteful to spend time découpaging screens. I would much rather attend the Royal Academy of Art, but I know females are not admitted. I read in Papa's paper that the government has established a Female School of Design, and when I am old enough perhaps I can attend it. However, I fear I am sadly lacking in artistic ability and no amount of tutoring can compensate for an absence of talent.

Most of all I would like to attend Cambridge, for then Mr. Austin-Brown and I could continue to have our dialogues. But then I know that to attend one of the colleges one must be male and a Christian. I am a Christian, but I can't make myself a boy.

I don't know what the future holds for me. If I had worked harder for Mr. Austin-Brown he might not have wished to leave.

I felt angry with Papa for taking Mr. Austin-Brown away, but then I chided myself for my selfish thoughts, for it is the fulfillment of his dreams. But I fear that Mr. Austin-Brown has a claim on my affections, and that my fancies have prevailed upon me a foolishness of spirit. I resolve to put my foolish notions to rest.

In spite of my resolution, as I fall asleep Mr. Austin-Brown remains on my mind. All his characteristics taken singly seem ordinary, but combined they evoke a feeling most disturbing.

I wonder if he will write me a letter. He didn't when he was gone before.

Dear Diary,

I feel a failure to the utmost, for yesterday I scorned my journal, failing in my vow to Mother, as well as myself, to record something of value every day. My malaise of spirit was such that I did not take pen to hand. Even when I tried to read a book that I usually find most thought-provoking, my mind was sadly laggard. I fear I have been prey to the sin of sloth. I even put Bridget off when she wished to pursue her letters.

My thoughts are so disturbed that I slept ill and awakened early, so am writing this in the pale light of dawn to keep my vow, to make up for my wasted yesterday. My spirits are in such lethargy that I had to make myself do it, and to feel better I determined to live up to my resolution to finish my sampler. Mother has a sampler she worked when she was even younger than I am, and her needlework is dainty enough for a fairy. I like the motto on her sampler that reads:

> *Give your love to your Creator*
> *Reverence to your superior*
> *Honour to your parents*
> *Your bosom to your friend*

But I know I could never work it as beautifully as she did. She suggested that I use a verse from Psalms for my work:

"When my father and my mother forsake me then the Lord will take me up."

Since I really don't find plying a needle a pleasure, I selected the shortest motto I could find for my sampler. I had already worked IDLE HANDS BREED MIS when I discovered I had no more brown thread in my workbox. As I needed matching brown thread sufficient to finish MISCHIEF, I went to look in the worktable Papa brought to Mother from Tunbridge Wells. It made me wish for Papa, for he and I frequently play backgammon on the game board of many fancy woods inlaid on the top of the table. Mother does not enjoy games. I think Papa hoped that such a lovely table would inspire her to learn to enjoy them. As I was rummaging through the threads I eyed a valentine, which I knew Papa sent to Mother, as she had once shown it to me. I decided to borrow it to use as a pattern for the stump work picture she wishes me to work on next.

The valentine has great beauty, with kissing lovebirds, garlands of flowers, Cupid with his bow and arrow, and a banner across the top with the words "The Endless Knot of Love." The Endless Knot itself Papa inscribed in his uneven sprawly script with a verse:

Love is a Virtue that endures forever,
A Link of Matchless Jewels none can sever,
They on whose breath this sacred love doth place,
Shall after death the fruits thereof embrace.

Among the many pleasures that we prove
None are so real as the Joys of Love
For this is Love and worth commending
Still beginning, never ending.

Mother had explained that the link of jewels encircling the knot, with its young Hercules at the top trying to pull apart the link, shows that true love is so firmly bound that even the god of strength cannot sever it.

I'm copying it here to remember, with the hope that some day I will have someone to whom to send such a verse. I am thinking of Mr. Austin-Brown as I write this. But Love must be returned for it to be True Love. I feel he holds me in high regard, but does he love me? Of course he cannot declare Love in his present impecunious condition.

I sketched the pattern, but it seems so very complicated for stump work. I plan to design the knot itself into my pattern and I hope to use the cupid, painting his face on silk and appliquéing it on the picture. I'll work the bow and arrow in thread.

When I opened the Valentine, a yellowed envelope addressed to Mother fell out. I knew it was from Papa because it is addressed in Papa's handwriting, and the sealing wax is impressed with the Primrose family crest, which Papa has on his ring. I know it is wrong to read another person's correspondence, so I shall return it to her worktable in the morning.

I was very disappointed that I did not have a letter from Mr. Austin-Brown today, but of course there has not been a sufficient passage of time. After I retired, Nanny brought me a letter from Papa, which arrived earlier in the day but she had forgotten to deliver to me. It brought the most distressing news. I am so concerned for Mother, and Papa must be beside himself. I cannot sleep because of my concern.

My Dear Little Cygnet,

Last evening at the dinner at Apsley House your mother felt faint and, much to my distress, swooned to the floor. Our host, the Duke of Wellington, immediately called for smelling salts, but we were unable to revive her.

I had such fear that she had contracted the cholera or typhoid.

Rest your fears, dear child. We rushed her across the road to the St. George's Hospital, knowing that there the finest care in the land is to be found.

She was finally revived, and, though the physicians are unable to say what her malady is, there is no fever and she does not have the plague, thanks be to God. They wished her to stay overnight for observation, so I insisted that I stay with her. I would not leave her alone in the hands of strangers.

This morning the physicians announced that they wish to perform surgery to relieve the pressure in her head, assuring me that these operations have been successfully performed even before St. George's opened in 1827. They assure me that they would use chloroform, which would save her from any pain. To give me more confidence, they told me that many women use chloroform in childbirth these days. Her Royal Highness took the chloroform when her last child was born. However, I have not yet agreed to the surgery, and hope that she will be sufficiently recovered so that we may return to our own abode, where she will be much happier in her own bedchamber.

I send this posthaste to let you know that our return will be delayed until her strength and health are recovered.

Your loving
Papa

Dear Diary,

I worried all morning about Papa and Mother, and penned a letter myself to give to the courier when he brings Papa's next letter. I asked permission to come to London to be with them. Late this afternoon I heard the metallic crunch of the gravel beneath the hooves of a horse, and then the sharp rapping of the great iron knocker on the front door. I rushed downstairs thinking it must be a letter for me from Papa or Mr. Austin-Brown. Alas, it was not, and to my great astonishment it proved to be for Bridget, so I took it upstairs to her. The courier could not take my letter to Papa, for he was not going to London.

Bridget opened the envelope and took out the letter, and turned it over several times with a look of puzzlement on her face. She then handed it to me commenting "I've never received a letter before. These little black marks don't mean a thing to me—please read it for me."

The letter was from the neighbour of her family in Ireland, and it bore the distressful news that her father had been arrested for killing a man who, though dressed as an English landowner, was indeed only a visitor to the city. This had caused her mother to have hysteria and a complete emotional collapse. As Bridget is the oldest child, she is needed to come home to care for the little children.

Bridget's face had become very white. The letter continued

My Dearest Wife,

I have missed you severely and regretted the necessity of such a long journey requiring my absence from your presence, especially at Christmastide.

How I wish you were here to enjoy with me the beauty of this island. There are mountains which overlook small lagoons with coral beaches. The flamboyant trees and lush tropical flowers thrive in this almost perfect climate. There is a unique geological feature called The Baths. The translucence of the seawater is like that of the Blue Grotto on Capri. I promise to take you there on the journey to Italy of which we have spoken.

I am giving this letter to one of the plantation owners who has been fortunate enough to secure passage on one of the new steamships, which is carrying his produce back to England. It is my expectation that you will receive it before I arrive home.

I have booked passage on a ship that is scheduled to depart next week. Hopefully God will provide favourable winds and the northerly course we will take will have us riding the currents. It is my prayer that our journey will take less than the fifty days it took on our westward journey.

The poor little motherless baby is stronger now and will be able to withstand the cold and rough seas we may experience.

My admiration for your generosity for taking in a little baby without a legitimate name, especially since you are expecting a babe of your own blood within a few months, makes me love you even more. I know you are doing this for me and for the reputation of the family name.

You will always be not only my moonbeam but also the sunlight in my life.

Your ever loving husband,
Godfrey

P.S. Tell Father that I am bringing him some of the best cigars he has ever smoked. And Cook will be thrilled with the supply of cayenne I will bring with me.

At first I was puzzled. But it soon became obvious. The motherless baby had to be me.

An overwhelming sorrow has engulfed me. To find I am not Mother's child at all!! No wonder I am such a disappointment to her. No wonder she has always been so formal and distant with me. I attributed it to her lack of strength, but instead she must have been ashamed of me. And Papa—I held him in the highest regard and love. He was never unkind to me, but it must have been because his conscience hurt him. He must be very ashamed of me and that is why he was always reluctant to take me anywhere. How could he have betrayed Mother this way? How could he have burdened her heart and her strength? It is so painful to think that he has lived a lie all these years. He is not the wonderful Papa I always thought he was. I trusted him. I never thought he would deceive me.

What a grievous revelation! My eyes are so bedimmed with tears that the words I write are blurred, but I must have someone to talk to. I no longer have Grandfather, nor Dearest Sister, and now even Mr. Austin-Brown is gone. And I will never be able to face him with this shameful knowledge. He would lose all respect for me.

I feel such mortification at this knowledge that my cheeks are burning with shame! How can I face Nanny or Crawford or Mrs. Potts? Nor anyone! I feel so ashamed I can never look Mother or Papa in the face again. I even feel shame to confide this to you, dear diary. I looked in the glass at the image facing me and asked, "Who are you?" But there was no answer, only a stranger looking back at me. I am cast in despair. I feel hollow and afraid, a deep absence inside of me. My very existence seems erased.

I am in a confusion as to my proper path.

Perhaps I should leave with Bridget and go to Ireland and help her and her family. Then maybe Papa could take pride in me. He admires Chef Soyer. I feel completely alone and useless. And Mr. Austin-Brown challenged me to transform my life into a life for others. I must prove to Papa and Mr. Austin-Brown that I am worthy of recognition—hopefully, even love. I have such perturbation of mind.

I don't know if I have the courage to leave and go where I know not what lies ahead. Everything will be different, and all won't be pleasant. I have no skills like Bridget does. I feel great trepidation when I realise that I may learn what it is to face hunger. But Bridget needs me. She is the only one who needs me, and she need never know this horrible secret. Perhaps God has a purpose for this discovery that seems so dreadful to me. Perhaps this is His will for me, and I should put my trust in Him and know that He will meet my needs. There must be happiness in alleviating someone else's sorrow. Perhaps I will be able to find meaning by losing myself.

I have great perplexity of thought. I am writing you, dear

diary, to better understand what course of action I should take.

I re-read the sentence above, and realised that I must pray to God to save me from a destructive course of action, and to put before me His vision for my life!

January 1992

And that was the last word in the journal. Only the backside of the last page remained empty.

I had so many questions. Had other eyes than mine seen these words since they were written? Was there another journal that followed this one? Did Cygnet accompany Bridget to Ireland, and what happened to all those to whom she had introduced me?

Knowing that the public library in Dallas has an excellent genealogy department, I scheduled a visit, hopeful that I could learn all I needed to know.

The helpful and knowledgeable librarian brought out their latest edition of *Debrett's Peerage and Baronetage*, dated 1990. The only listing under the name Primrose was a Scottish peer, the Earl of Rosebery, whose family home since 1817 has been Dalheny House near Edinburgh. Even a careful perusal of the listed predecessors going all the way back to 1651 did not reveal a possible relative. Most conclusively, the family crest was quite different from that on the cover of the journal.

But the librarian suggested several other sources. The first to help me in my quest was entitled *Alumni Cantabrigiensis: A Biographical List of All Known Students, Graduates and Holders of Office at the University of Cambridge from the Earliest Times Until 1980.* It was exciting to find the listing:

> Primrose, William Henry, 5th Brt. of Chatfield, 1782–1846. S. of William Godfrey Primrose, 4th Brt. of Chatfield, adm. pens. (age 19) at Trinity, 1801, Matric. Michs. 1802, B.A. in classics 1804, M.A. 1808. M.P. 1820–1834. Married and had children. Died Oct. 30, 1846, and buried at Primrose family graveyard at St. Michael's Church, Chatfield.

It seemed much too brief a listing for Cygnet's beloved Grandfather, a person for whom I had developed great admiration.

Knowing that Mr. Austin-Brown attended Cambridge, I eagerly scanned the volume containing those names starting with A. When my eyes saw "Austin-Brown, John," a thrill ran up my spine. And here is exactly how he was cited in the book:

> Austin-Brown, John. adm. sizar (age 20) at King's September, 1848. Matric. Michs. 1848; Chancellor's Medal for English verse 1849; Scholar 1850; B.A. in classics 1852.

Fellow 1852–1854. Buried in Mill Road Cemetery, Cambridge (King's Coll., Adm Reg: A1Oxon).

This information left me with my interest only more piqued. Did he marry? Have children? When did he die? Unfortunately many of the entries of this time period were inconsistent or incomplete, and though it was a pleasure to discover his name, his entry left me frustrated.

Next we consulted *The Concise Dictionary of National Biography from Earliest Times to 1985*. We were so pleased to find Papa listed but surprised to see the word *extinct* after his name:

> Primrose, William Godfrey, 6th Brt. of Chatfield 1808–1864. S. of William Henry Primrose, 5th Brt. of Chatfield. Educated at Eton and Trinity. Landowner famous for his development of a shorthorn herd, a magistrate in Chatfield 1840–1851, M.P. 1851–1860, Patron of the livings of Chatfield and Westfield. Married and had son and daughter. Died April 24, 1864. Buried at St. Michael's Church at Primrose Hall. *extinct*

Only one daughter!! *The Concise Dictionary* was too concise indeed.

As Vivian and I planned a return visit to London with a group of friends for the opening celebration of The Lanesborough, we vowed to work further research into the crowded schedule of activities.

Riding from Gatwick Airport in the hotel's chauffeured car, we were thrilled to pass Buckingham Palace at the moment of the changing of the guard. Only perhaps two hundred yards farther, as we circled the Constitution Arch, we saw the Household Cavalry on their perfectly matched shining black horses, with their red-coated uniforms and white-tasseled helmets, passing beneath the Arch. "How wise the British are to preserve their pageantry," Vivian remarked. Across the busy thoroughfare was a limestone building in pristine condition, and glancing up I could see the words ST. GEORGE'S HOSPITAL chiseled in the façade.

We entered The Lanesborough's driveway, and a smartly uniformed doorman welcomed us all smiles beneath his derby hat. Waiting to greet us was the managing director, Geoffrey Gelardi, an old friend who had worked in Dallas for Rosewood Hotels & Resorts shortly after The Mansion on Turtle Creek was opened. A British citizen and son of a famous hotelier, he had grown up in hotels, and we thought him the ideal choice as manager of The Lanesborough.

In a fireplace located directly past the entrance doors a cheery fire burned brightly. I was pleased with the ambience of the hotel, intimate yet elegant, formal yet comfortable. We were shown to our rooms without further delay.

I went to the bedroom window to examine my view. Though the street was heavy with traffic, the room was very quiet. I looked across to the ornamental Hyde Park Arch and to Apsley House, the home of the Duke of Wellington, which was presented to him in appreciation for his victory at Waterloo. In my mind's eye, I thought of the dinner party described by Papa in his letter to Cygnet, and visualized her mother being carried across the road, possibly into the very room in which I was standing.

Our first day's excursion took us to Bath, where we were to meet a friend staying at the hotel in the Royal Crescent. I was particularly interested in seeing The Crescent, since Philip Johnson, the architect of The Crescent in Dallas, where Rosewood's Hotel Crescent Court is located, had told me that his inspiration for the complex had come from the Royal Crescent in Bath.

When I telephoned my friend to invite her to meet us for lunch, I was interested to learn that she was staying in the Beau Nash suite. We had named the restaurant in the Hotel Crescent Court the Beau Nash after the famed bon vivant and social lion of eighteenth-century Bath. When we arrived she took us to visit the Baths, which date back to the days of Roman occupation, stopped in an antique mall housed in an old church, and had a most enjoyable day with all our friends. We arrived back at The Lanesborough just in time to prepare for dinner.

The next day, as we were free of scheduled activities, Vivian and I seized the opportunity to visit a country house where we had previously purchased a wonderful eighteenth-century clock. As the house lay in the direction of Primrose Hall, we also wanted to revisit the home of our little Cygnet. (If the truth be known, the return to Primrose Hall was by far the more important destination to me.)

The gates to Primrose Hall were open, and in the field a number of vehicles belonging to workmen were parked. The house itself was under renovation for its new owners, an American family from New York.

We were disappointed to find the doors to the tiny church locked, so we contented ourselves with looking at the headstones and taking notes. We walked toward the two tallest monuments. One had a beautifully carved angel with outspread wings. The base was inscribed:

PRIMROSE

AMY ELIZABETH

June 30, 1834–November 16, 1847

Our Angel on Earth Is Now
An Angel in Heaven

Next to her grave the other monument was inscribed:

PRIMROSE
WILLIAM HENRY
Lt. Fifth Regiment
Royal Grenadiers
Died
Madras, India
April 3, 1843–June 16, 1864

Because he died so young, we discussed the possibilities that his death had resulted from a military action combating a native uprising or from some foreign illness.

Two graves lying side by side with a common headstone, read:

PRIMROSE
WILLIAM GODFREY   AMY CAMILLA
May 1, 1808–December 24, 1864   May 2, 1810–October 29, 1848

This information told us that William's death had occurred only five months before Papa's death; and that his mother had died only three weeks after the last entry in Cygnet's diary. We wondered if Papa had agreed to the surgery.

We took notes of all the graves with the Primrose name but

found none with the date of 1833, the year of Cygnet's birth. The mystery and our curiosity only grew deeper.

The hour necessitated our departure, as we had a three-hour drive back to London and would arrive barely in time to join our group for dinner at The Lanesborough. After dinner I stayed up half the night preparing a family tree of the Primrose family from all the notes I had taken, correlating them with the facts as related in the journal. It was clear I had developed an obsession with the Primrose family.

The following day our excursion took us to Kew Gardens. Though Vivian and I had anticipated visiting the Palm Court, we found it closed for restoration. The smokestack tower had been razed many years prior. As we had a little free time before our evening activities, we had our tour bus drop us off at the Public Records Office in Kew. An attendant directed us to the Enquiry Office, where our Reader's Tickets were to be obtained; our passports satisfied the Keeper of Public Records that we were suitable for access to the records, and we were directed to the Langdale Reading Room.

The young woman at the distribution counter there greeted us, assigned us seats, and issued us a beeper, with the assurance that a member of the staff would advise us. Finally, a bespectacled librarian approached us, listened to our requests, but explained that only three microfilmed documents at a time could be issued to us; moreover, no records could be checked out after 4:15 P.M. The clock read 4:12 P.M. Then he explained that the Kew office housed only the records of the Cabinet, the Treasury back to the sixteenth century, the Admiralty, the Foreign Office, and the War Office. As an alternative he suggested we might more easily find what we were seeking at the Public Records Office on Chancery Lane.

Taking pity on our sorrowful reaction after having come such a long way, he agreed to bring out the limit of three microfilms from the War Office but needed to know the regiment in which we were interested. Having learned from William's tombstone that he was a lieutenant in the Fifth Battalion, Royal Grenadiers, Madras in 1864, we sent him searching. Though we were racing the clock, we were awed to find references to William Henry Primrose, born April 3, 1843, attached to the Fifth Battalion, Madras, India—killed by a tiger, June 16, 1864. His records detailed that he had received prior reprimand for forays into the forest for personal reasons. But it also noted that as a scientist he had identified sixty hitherto unidentified beetles and been nominated for an award from the Royal Entomology Society. Vivian and I wondered whether William's fascination with the lowly beetle or his curiosity about the noble tiger caused his death.

Our own foray to the Kew Records Office was time well spent, even if we had forgone the time we could have devoted to making our hair more presentable for dinner.

That night we celebrated in the Conservatory Room at The Lanesborough. In the renovation, the courtyard of the hospital had been enclosed in glass, its decor inspired by the Royal Pavilion at Brighton. There was music and dancing, as well as a very special menu prepared by Chef Gayler. One of the more adventurous members of our group approached our table and requested a dance with the guest of honor, Mrs. Margaret Thatcher. In surprise, she exclaimed that no one had invited her to dance in years, and, yes, she would take a turn around the room.

Our group was totally occupied the next day with a visit to the Queen's Library at Windsor Castle. Our farewell dinner was another delicious meal featuring beef Wellington and ending with an indulgent cappuccino crème brûlée served in a demitasse cup.

The next morning, after bidding our friends adieu, we hastened to the Public Records Office on Chancery Lane near Fleet Street. Our ticket from Kew secured us entry. The attendant looked discouraged when we told him we were looking for records of a female by the name of Primrose whose given name we did not know. We hastened to assure him that we did know the names of her parents and her birth date, August 24, 1833.

He patiently explained that until 1837 there was no provision for the central registration of births, marriages, and deaths in England and that records before that date are usually held by the registrar of the diocese of the Church of England in the appropriate parish. He looked in his book *Record Repositories in Great Britain* for the diocese of Hereford. When we told him we had just returned from that area, he advised us to telephone the diocese and put in our inquiry. The helpful attendant even provided us with the proper coin for the pay phone, and talked to the registrar of Hereford himself.

The call was worthwhile. Hereford did have entries of the births of Papa, William Godfrey Primrose, in 1808 and of his sister Emma Amelia at Primrose Hall, Chatfield, in 1807. Also recorded was his marriage to Amy Camilla Genevers on May 1, 1831. And, yes, there were two children born to the union: Amy Elizabeth, born June 30, 1834, and died November 16, 1847, and William Henry, born April 3, 1843, and died June 16, 1864—both buried in the Primrose family graveyard at St. Michael's Church, Chatfield.

When he noted that we were puzzled by this news, we explained that we had acquired a journal written presumably by a third child of William Godfrey Primrose. We couldn't understand why she would not be listed. His face lit up, and he suggested that if she lived at Primrose Hall she would be on the census roll of 1841. The 1841 census was the first to include names, ages, sex, and occupation, though not the relationships between members of a household. He suggested that we go to the Census Search Room in the Land Registry Building on Portugal Street. Forgetting all about lunch, we hailed a cab and headed directly there.

To facilitate our search we immediately engaged someone to help us search the census records for Chatfield and Primrose Hall. And, finally, we found our Little Cygnet. Listed as a member of the household in 1841 was Amelia Ann Primrose, age nine, female. Amy Elizabeth's and William's places of birth were listed as Primrose Hall—but our Cygnet's place of birth was noted as "at sea."

We wanted to know more, of course, but the clerk informed us that the records of the Registrar General of Shipping and Seamen dated back only to 1854; our search—for now—was at an end.

Caught up in the preparations for the return trip, we had run out of time for further research in England. However, once we settled into our seats for the ten-hour flight back to Dallas, we immediately re-read the journal and our notes about the Primrose family. Our Cygnet bore family names—Ann, the name of Papa's own mother, and Amelia, that of Papa's sister, who had gone to the West Indies to be married, only to find her fiancé had died of yellow fever.

Was she the child of Emma Amelia, whom Papa called Swan, and her deceased fiancé, whose name remained unknown? The re-reading of the journal had given us many clues, not the least of which was her nickname: Little Cygnet.

Vivian and I felt certain that Cygnet had made the wrong assumption as to her parentage. The obvious close bond between the child and her "Papa" must have made it inconceivable to her that he was not her father. If indeed her birth was illegitimate, as we guessed, she was truly Emma Amelia's child—the little Swan, the Cygnet. She would naturally have been given the family name of Primrose; and her mother's true identity would never have been disclosed to the world.

We could not be certain whether Cygnet accompanied Bridget to Ireland and whether Lettuce went with them. If she did, we felt Papa would have gone to find her. Or, if he was unable to leave London because of his wife's illness, he would have sent someone in his place. Would she and Bridget have reached Ireland safely? If she returned, why was she not buried in the Primrose family graveyard? *Debrett's* indicated that the baronetage had become extinct. According to the family tree we had been able to assemble, William had predeceased Papa; Papa must have been left without male relatives by whom the title would be inherited. Or is it possible he disowned his title?

We are eager to learn what happened to her, even if it becomes a lifelong search. Will we discover more about our Cygnet, this endearing young woman we now know as Amelia Ann, the young Lady Primrose?

We will try. But no matter, we know we love her—whoever she is.

Primrose Family Tree

(compiled from author's research)

3rd Baronet of Chatfield
Great-Great-Grandfather
PRIMROSE, William Henry

1710–1772
married 1736
Emma Amelia Tyson
1715–1748

4th Baronet of Chatfield
Great-Grandfather
PRIMROSE, William Godfrey

1738–1789
married 1772
Jane Mary Brockton
1748–1788

George Henry
1740–1761
(killed in duel)

(The Ghost)
1737–1748
(suicide)

5th Baronet of Chatfield
"Grandfather"
PRIMROSE, William Henry
1782–1846
married 1803
Elizabeth Ann Stanton
1784–1808

Godfrey George
1789–1813
(killed Trafalgar)

John Richard
1785–1815
(killed Battle of Waterloo)

6th Baronet of Chatfield
"Papa"
PRIMROSE, William Godfrey
May 1, 1808–December 24, 1864
married May 1, 1831
Amy Camilla Genevers
May 2, 1810–October 29, 1848

"Swan"
Emma Amelia
January 8, 1807–
September 1833
(died in West Indies)

Henry Richard
1811–1826
(killed shotgun accident)

"Little Angel"
Amy Elizabeth
June 30, 1834–November 16, 1847

"Little Cygnet"
Amelia Ann
August 24, 1833–??

"Soldier"
William Henry
April 30, 1843–June 16, 1864
(soldier killed in India)

All information about historical persons is accurate. Any resemblance of the Primrose Hall characters to persons living or dead is purely coincidental.

In appreciation for their love I dedicate this book to all my family.

I appreciate the contribution of Papa's poem by Charles Simmons and the inspiration, the encouragement, the research assistants, the computer skills, the legal advice, the editing provided by

Lloyd Bockstruck

Victoria Bogner

Anne Browning

Bob Compton

Peter Deison

Evan Fogelman

Charlene Howell

Lannie Johansen

Schuyler Marshall

Cal Morgan

Shirley Pieratt

Charles Simmons

Kurth Sprague

Fran Vick

Virginia Yancey

Vivian Young and

Barbara Wedgwood.

About the Author

CAROLINE ROSE HUNT, creator and honorary chairman of Rosewood Hotels & Resorts, was named one of the most powerful women in the travel industry by *Travel Agent* magazine in 1999.

An owner of Lady Primrose's Antique Store, she is the creator of Lady Primrose's Royal Bathing Luxuries, a line of products found in exclusive hotels and stores around the world. From 1985 to 1995 she was a presidential appointee to the Board of Trustees of the John F. Kennedy Center for the Performing Arts, and she has been named one of America's 100 Most Influential Women by *Ladies' Home Journal*.

Ms. Hunt is a graduate of Mary Baldwin College and holds a degree in English literature from the University of Texas. The mother of five children, she is a certified instructor in Parent Effectiveness Training. *Primrose Past* is her first novel.